Sandy Austrin-Miner v
graduated and worked in
overland to Scotland when

She has previously pul   .... .s
Love", for which she was awarded the Silver Award in the
category of Best Novel of 2005 by the Christian Broadcasting
Council.

She presently lives outside of Edinburgh as a fulltime
mother to her four children, writing as family demands
permit.

Sandy Austrin-Miner

Glimpses

Latent Publishing

British Library Cataloguing in Publication Data

A catalogue record for this book is available from the
British Library.

ISBN 0-9548821-1-3

Printed and Bound in Scotland.

Dedicated to my husband, Sam,
whose steadfast support and
encouragement has made
this book possible.

Sx.

GLIMPSES

CONTENTS

Of a Bride

She gazed sadly at the familiar portrait. The sepia faces of her grandparents had stared fixedly into the disused entrance hall all her childhood: hand-tinted eyes unnaturally blue, cheeks glowing too warmly. It had been the fashion to colour radiance into the bride's smooth-skinned face, and pinken the grey tones of her bouquet. Lace fell in simple folds over her grandmother's slender form as she stood tall and sure on her grandfather's youthful arm.

Time had brought the babble and rush of several waves of children through this house, and had left it again, quiet and still; emptiness settling over the dusty ornaments and faded photographs; grandmother stooped and lined; grandfather's tomb bleaching in the sun.

The wedding photo had hung invisibly throughout her growing years, unobtrusive amongst the clutter that defined her grandparents' house; china ornaments and miniature jugs, tapestry scenes and sprays of dried flowers; great Aunts peering sternly from silver frames. Each object had been examined by little-girl eyes, but had now grown indistinct and lost in the half-lit halls and memories.

It now glared accusingly, pricking regret, stinging her conscience. Tears ached and swelled in her dry throat. Through the yellowing photograph she saw her grandmother's youth wrapped in silk, white and pure; her innocence gazing softly from the folds of lace. Grandfather was clothed in confidence and respectability as he led his shining bride to the camera, their bright faces captured for future generations.

Friends clucked noisily around her. Dread hung on her exhausted heart.

"Isn't it wonderful to be planning a wedding! So exciting!"

She felt nausea welling up and looked silently away. The excited chatter droned on as a distant, sickening hum. Her heart drummed anxiously. She felt them tugging at her, trying to pull her into the conversation. She struggled dismally to feign an interest in flowers and bows, then sank back into her silence. Baffled, her friends shifted the conversation away from her, stepping around her misery. The chatter babbled on annoyingly around her.

Cars hummed impatiently along the busy street. Shoppers pressed along the crowded pavements, arms draped with swinging bags. She hesitated in front of a large shop window, glancing nervously around. She slid noiselessly through the shop door and moved self-consciously across the floor, straining to be invisible, feeling the eyes of the attendant burning against her. She felt shabby and worn amongst the rails of gleaming white dresses. She fumbled and sweated. She longed to rush out into the cool air of the street, but remained inside, hot and unsteady. Nervously she slid gowns along the rails, sweeping her eyes over them uncomfortably. Coat-hangers scraped and screeched against the metal rails, shattering the heavy silence of the shop. The strain grew unbearable and, in a flustered paroxysm, she lunged for the door, bursting out into the fresh air.

Basking in the relief of space and anonymity, she lounged in front of the shop window, finding the confidence to look at the display. A mannequin, draped in wedding silk, leaned in sylph-like elegance among roses, gazing tranquilly beyond the passing shoppers. As she looked on, her aching sadness swelled and spilled over her cheeks as hot tears. She turned and hurried away.

The wedding day approached with a sickening sense of dread. She procrastinated anxiously about every arrangement. Lists haunted her; she felt paralysed with indecision.

"Can't we just elope?" she suggested weakly.

Her betrothed smiled. "Have to keep the family happy, I suppose. Everyone is waiting to see you walk down the aisle looking beautiful."

She shuddered. She saw herself in a white dress, its brilliance fading and yellowing as she moved towards the altar, till she arrived, stained and worn; crimsoned by her lie.

She became irritable and withdrawn; he was baffled and hurt. Silence gripped them both as they groped around in the emotions that separated them. She seemed to be shrouded in a cold misery; he grew urgent.

"What's happening? Please speak to me," he begged.

She looked at him through weary eyes, seeing him struggling in his pain. She grasped at the scraps of explanation that jostled around in her mind, struggling to make them into words which would comfort him, but she felt trapped in her silence. Shame flooded through her cheeks and burned, pressing her eyes to the floor.

Face still averted, she squeezed out a whispered confession. "It will be a lie to wear white." Sweat pricked her humiliation.

His face creased with confusion. "What do you mean? I still don't understand." She heard despair creep into his voice.

"I'm not white," she mumbled, her voice sinking, "so how can I wear a white dress? But everyone is expecting it. I'm trapped."

He looked at the pain that blanched her face and understood. He lifted her tear-soaked face and spoke gently to her. "I have already forgiven you for everything. You are "white" to me; like you have never known another man." He paused thoughtfully before he continued. "I'll get you a dress; leave it to me."

Alarmed, she spluttered with objections. "You can't do that. That's not right."

He smoothed back fallen strands of hair and reassured her.

"Trust me. It will be the right dress."

As time moved stealthily forward, lingering over each day, doubt still shadowed and tormented her. She ruminated over his words, his promise, trying to trust. Maybe he hadn't really understood. He certainly knew all about her. She winced as memories flamed and scorched her conscience. Happiness quietly grew in him as it drained from her.

The day arrived. She sat pensively before the mirror, trying to brush colour into her pale face, shivering in her dressing gown and thin slip, poking disinterested strands of hair into soft braids. She waited for the clock to strike, minutes beating steadily into the stillness. The door latch clicked and his face appeared silently in the mirror above hers. The hour chimed noisily.

"I have the dress," he smiled.

She nodded mutely.

"Close your eyes."

She obeyed. She felt him gently guide her to her feet and listened to the rustle of tissue paper. Her dressing gown tumbled from her shoulders as light fabric floated like a veil over her face and fell about her figure, brushing her feet with its hem.

"Don't look yet."

She felt his breath warm on her neck as he whispered gently through the darkness to her.

"Husbands, love your wives, just as Christ loved the church and gave himself up for her to make her holy, cleansing her by the washing of water through the word, so that he might present her to himself in splendour, without stain or any other blemish, but holy and blameless."

His breath slid silently away.

"You can open your eyes now."

She lifted her hesitant lids and turned her eyes to the mirror. He was gone. Pain shot through her heart but then she caught her own reflection and was held in breathless wonder. An image of trailing white floated before her. Soft tears tumbled painlessly down her cheeks, melting the icy fear of the past months. She smiled through her glistening tears.

She hurried across the churchyard, unaware of the sharp thrusts of wind that tugged at her hair, scattering stones from the gravel path. Her father followed in steady formality, his shoes crunching a deliberate step. She waited, panting, in the portico. Snatching her father's arm as the heavy, wooden doors were pushed open, she stepped boldly into the aisle to the heavy chimes of organ; a sea of faces straining towards her.

She rested her gaze on him; his face turned expectantly towards her, eyes gleaming with a beckoning smile, drawing her to him. She stepped in rustling silk up to his side. His voice reached softly towards her.

"I love you."

In a moment the stream of hymns and vows had passed and she was hurrying back up the aisle, arm buried in his, through a crowd swaying with emotion. They emerged suddenly from the dimly lit church and stepped blinking into the bright sunlight, surprised by cameras. She leaned into her husband's side, her dress ballooning in the wind, billowing in brilliant whiteness against the dark, arched doorway. The couple stepped laughingly towards the clicking cameras, as they flashed and framed the scene for future generations.

Rejoice and be glad,
For the wedding day of the Lamb has come.
And His bride has made herself ready,
Fine linen, bright and pure,
Was given her to wear.

Revelation 19:7&8

GLIMPSES

Beneath the surface

She hurried along the jetty, the sun glinting on her loose, blonde curls which swung restlessly. Her darting eyes searched nervously, almost unaware of the flawless blue sky which domed her, and the myriad of smooth white gulls which soared and reeled gracefully around her, circling and diving through the clear air. Salt smarted in her nostrils as she drew each panting breath, squeezing air into her tight chest. Her feet skipped unevenly over the wooden planks that spanned the jetty, tripping over coils of rope, winding around nets strewn in tangled mounds and bundles of oyster pots dotted with brightly coloured floats. Her face was pinched into an expression of anxiety as she squinted against the bright sun. The caw, calling of gulls which rang and floated through the sky, merged with the slap of waves as they beat rhythmically against the worn, wooden timbers and the gentle "tink, tink" of the rocking boats. Her eyes scanned the rows of gleaming yachts moored to the wooden jetty as she hurried along.

Her chest rising and falling with quick breaths, she stopped and cast her eyes over the deck of one yacht as it bobbed lazily, rocked by the small, lapping waves. She gazed thoughtfully at the bodies strewn over the deck. One by one they raised their heads, blinking and shading their eyes from the intense sun as they took a squinting look at her.

Jade, her slender figure stretched out on a towel, viewed the young woman through reflective glasses which carefully obscured her observant eyes and mirrored the world in bulbous distortion. She dropped her head back, her lipsticked mouth pouting to the sky, her bronze body drinking in the sun, her long, slender arm trailing a half empty wine glass. Her voice yawned, deep and honeyed.

"You're two hours late!"

Flustered, Prisca sat up quickly, smoothing the folds of her skirt.

"Vanessa, what on earth has happened? The morning is half over! You know we were all meeting at nine. We've all been worried about you. How could you do this to us? It's such a perfect day for sailing, and so far we've just sat in the marina."

"It's not been so terribly unpleasant," Drew's smooth voice oiled rich and deep as he swirled his glinting wine around its crystal glass, and cast his appreciative eye over the draped figures of Jade and Prisca. He tilted his head back, and languidly poured the sweet liquid into his mouth. "Still, glad you've made it; it wouldn't have been a party without you. I think we could do with a bit of brightening up!"

Vanessa stood staring at them uncertainly from the jetty.

"Well, come on, climb aboard." Prisca's voice was sharp and impatient. Then softer, she continued,

"Are you alright Vee? You look pale. Definitely not yourself. What is it? "

"I'm sorry I'm late," Vanessa stammered. "Something really awful's happened." Suddenly she shivered and swayed unsteadily.

"Oh!" squealed Prisca, "she's going to faint."

"I'm not going to faint," Vanessa replied sharply, "but I do feel quite sick and light headed."

Drew raised himself up on his elbows and examined her. "Still look gorgeous to me, but allow me to be your rescuer," he answered laughingly. He sat up and swung his tanned and muscular legs to the ground. Easing himself up, he settled his glass, and sauntered across to the side of the boat. "Fall into my arms and I'll save you." A ring of laughter circled the boat.

Vanessa stretched out her hand to take the one Drew was offering her. His grip was strong and reassuring; she let him guide her into the boat and steady her feet on the deck. As she withdrew her hand, he circled his arms around her. "And now let me kiss you." A roar of laughter broke out behind him as the girls convulsed with giggles.

"Go away, Drew," Vanessa snapped and pushed him away in irritation, leaning back to avoid his searching lips.

"Unhand that woman, you cad. Release her, I say."

"James! Have you finished playing with your ropes?" Jade's sultry voice rang sarcastically.

James clambered across the yacht. "Well, somebody has to do the work," he replied defensively. "You're here, Vee. Excellent! Now where's Mark?"

"Unconscious," replied Vanessa sharply.

"Unconscious!" several voices exclaimed.

"When I last saw him." Her last image of Mark flashed vividly across her mind; him sprawled across their untidy bed, reeking of alcohol and cigarette smoke, snoring off a hang-over. With a smouldering sense of anger and hopeless disappointment, she had flung her things into a bag and charged off with plenty of time to meet her friends.

"Now, that is a disappointment. Mark is an excellent yachtsman; I really needed his help," James moaned.

"And an excellent drinker, I must add. But I shall struggle on without his assistance, no doubt." Drew rolled his eyes to imitate James and amuse the girls. They sniggered responsively.

"Well, you young ladies will have to take your turn at the till," concluded James. A chorus of moans followed.

"So, what dreadful thing happened to you to then?" Jade's treacle voice enquired in a tone of mock concern.

Vanessa shuddered as she reflected on the morning's events. She sat down on the end of Jade's towel, forcing her to draw her legs up to make space. Jade scowled playfully and moved her feet.

"Do you like my nail-polish?" she asked, examining her well tanned feet.

"Jade!" Prisca hissed in annoyance. "We are trying to find out what happened to Vee. Now tell us Vee, what happened?"

With obvious effort, Vee recalled the morning. How, after finding that she couldn't rouse Mark, she had left the house bristling with anger, rehearsing what she would say to him, picturing with satisfaction his disappointment when he discovered she had gone. Her mind had been boiling with how she was going to punish him.

"All I remember is suddenly hearing the screech of tyres and looking up. The car was almost on me. I could see the face of the driver screaming; hear the horn blasting but I couldn't move. I was frozen, waiting for it to hit. But it didn't! With a thump which winded me," Vanessa's voice shook with tears, "I was pushed out of the way."

"Pushed out of the way!" the enthralled voices echoed. "By who?"

"By a man." Vanessa broke into sobs which convulsed her slight body. "He pushed me out of the way and was hit by the car instead."

A shocked silence fell over the group, broken by the muffled tears of Vanessa, and the constant, rocking "tink, tink" of the rigging.

"What happened to him?" Jade asked seriously.

Vanessa's tears gushed loudly. She struggled to answer. "He was hurt badly; I don't know how bad; he looked awful; covered in blood."

"So, who is he? Do you know him? A secret admirer?" Drew enquired provocatively.

"No!" Vanessa retorted. "I'd never seen him before. I don't know who he is."

"Your guardian angel, I should think," added Prisca.

Vanessa gave her a scathing look. "I don't know why a total stranger would throw himself in front of a car to save me. It doesn't make sense."

"Chivalry is not dead, my dear."

"Drew! That is an idiotic remark. Be quiet if you have nothing sensible to say," Prisca scolded him.

Jade had been silent. "You're right. It doesn't make sense. Why sacrifice yourself; even for someone you love... but for a stranger?"

"Did you speak to him?" James asked.

"I just kept blubbering that I was sorry; so sorry. He just moaned with pain." Vee's voice wavered and fell silent.

They all looked at each other uncomfortably; perplexed.

"I think we all need another drink," Drew mumbled awkwardly, and grasping the wine bottle by the neck, he splashed wine into everyone's glass.

"A glass for you, my dear, to clear you mind and improve your disposition," he said, thrusting a glass into Vee's trembling hand. "A toast," he called. "Raise your glasses to friends and a good day of sailing."

Sun light sparkled on the glass rims and swirling wine, caressing their upturned faces and smiling on their youth and beauty.

"Now, let's get this boat moving. Vee, I think you should sit there for a while. Gather yourself." James' voice was deep with concern. "But I'll need everyone else to help."

Vanessa shrunk into a sunny corner of the deck, hugging her knees and sipping wine, as her languid companions eased themselves into activity. Shouts and giggles wafted across her thoughts, carried by the light breeze that cooled the steady beating sun. A cold sense of horror still gripped her as the boat slowly edged away from the creaking timber jetty, and manoeuvred its way through the rows of moored yachts, rocking and rising on the lapping waves.

She could hear Drew's constant playful banter, flirting and teasing; Jade's cool, sarcastic retorts as she moved, sleek as a cat, around the boat; Prisca's voice ringing in search of praise; James trying to instil a sense of seriousness, his voice taut with exasperation. Vanessa hugged herself tighter, shrinking away from their frothy laughter and light affections. The sun crept warm and delicious across her chilled skin, the cool sips of the wine spread like a cosy blanket through her mind, muffling the haunting scream. But at her core she was sick and trembling, as over and over she felt the dull thud of being pushed aside, and saw the car slamming into that man.

Tilting her head back, she watched the flapping, white sail edge its way up the mast, and stretch into an arc, taut against the wind. James' voice snapped orders; feet scrambled over the deck. With a pull, Vanessa felt the wind grasp the sails and lurch the boat forward in a rush of salty spray. The yacht rose and fell as they surged through the choppy waves and whistled through the wind. Vanessa could feel the tension slipping from her worn face and her heart wanting to rush through the great, green basin of sea; like the bow of the yacht as it sliced through the rolling waves.

A figure dropped lightly to her side, breaking her dreamy thoughts. "I can almost see a smile. The sea has captured your heart!"

"Drew! Where did you spring from?" Vanessa was startled.

"I'm never far away. Keeping my eye on you. And it's a very pleasant occupation, I confess." Drew stretched himself out beside Vanessa, propped on his elbow. With his head resting on his hand, he leant towards her, smiling. "I'm worried about you. You've had a big fright."

Vanessa felt herself shrink away, confused by his solemnity.

"You're going to tease me again, aren't you."

"No!" he exclaimed self righteously, looking wounded. "I care about you."

Vanessa examined him cautiously, aware of his eyes fixed on her, conscious of her discomfort. Words seemed impossibly distant, so she looked out at the stretch of sea that was widening between them and the low strip of green shore.

The sun rolled over them in soporific waves, dulling her thoughts and pressing heavily on her eyelids. The silence stretched awkwardly between them. Vanessa's folded body was tense with expectation, dreading Drew's flirtatious comments. Drew's face was crossed with emotion. Vanessa kept her eyes fixed on the shrinking shoreline. Drew's voice broke uncertainly into the stiff silence.

"So, you and Mark had a big night last night?"

Vanessa faltered at the change in Drew's normally buoyant voice. Her eyes flashed sideways, catching a glimpse of his altered face.

"Mark had a big night," she answered cautiously.

"You weren't out together then?"

"No." The questions irritated her and she wondered where they were leading. She was still uncomfortably aware of Drew's figure inclined towards her, his hand so close to her arm that her skin prickled. She felt herself trying to edge invisibly away. Something in Drew's serious tone disturbed her more than his jesting.

"You're wasting yourself on him." Drew's voice was small and tight.

Vanessa groaned silently with alarm and recoiled inwardly. She had been dodging Drew's searching looks and suggestive words for years, but she couldn't face a serious talk now. Hurt and disappointment were so fresh in her heart, it was hard to pretend that she was happy. She stiffened her emotions with a smile, and shrugged off his remark.

"So, I should waste myself on you instead?"

Drew looked shocked at her stinging remark. He was used to her blushing sweetness. His face hardened. He smoothed away his emotion and restored his flawless, handsome expression; gathering his mouth into a smooth, confident smile, ready to sling a cool remark back.

"Well, we shall have to get a few more glasses of wine in, if we are going to catch up with your boyfriend." His voice rang shallow with bitterness. "Excuse me while I attend to my guests."

Vanessa watched him ease himself away, twirling the stem of his glass in his fingers, grasping the champagne bottle by its neck.

"Refreshments! Allow me to refresh your glass." Drew's strong voice rang into the salty wind and was muffled by the beating of canvas as the sails flapped and stretched.

"Are you going to do any work today?" James' voice was soon lost in the cheers and laughter as the friends picked up their glasses.

Vanessa rested her head and closed her eyes as she listened to the soothing sounds of wind and boat, the sun a fiery ball overhead, the icy sea spray startling her from time to time. She tried to glide with the racing boat but her thoughts were tangled and threatening. Dread crept like a chill into her heart.

She gazed up into the arching bowl of blue that stretched to the almost disappearing strip of land and merged with the deepening hues of the sea, and she was struck by her smallness. The vast expanse of sea enlarged around her, dwarfing the vessel that was now tossed and thrown by the heaving waters, and driven by winds that hurtled across the ocean's surface. She thought of the depths beneath her, the fathoms of darkness, the massive volumes; herself a cork, bobbing precariously. Flooded with reality, Vanessa gasped and rushed away from her musings. She sprang unsteadily to her feet and, staggering a little, she clambered towards her friends and their giddy laughter.

Vanessa found them lounging sleepily on the deck, the smell of sun-tan lotion mingling with salt spray. She settled hesitantly among them and circled the group with her eyes. Prisca placed her book down carefully and looked at Vanessa.

"Are you alright?"

Vanessa nodded and diverted her eyes from Prisca's enquiring face.

"Is it lunchtime?" Vanessa asked after some time, trying to make her question sound light.

"If you're volunteering to get lunch, then it must be." Drew had regained his usual swagger.

Vanessa grasped the opportunity and leapt lightly up.

"We'll have a picnic!"

She disappeared into the small cabin and could be heard searching cupboards. The others exchanged questioning looks.

"Is she alright?" James asked in a hoarse whisper.

"I don't really know," Prisca mouthed back. "She hasn't said anything to me."

"What a strange story. Do you think it's true?" Jade's voice was cool and clear.

"Shsh! She'll hear you. Of course it's true. Vee doesn't make things up. It's obviously really shaken her up." Prisca went on, trying to keep her voice low, but wanting to make use of the opportunity to talk. "It's just so bizarre. Somebody who doesn't know her, risking his life to save her."

"He probably didn't think about it. Just jumped instinctively," reasoned James. "Just noticed her stepping in front of the car and tried to grab her."

"It's still heroic, even if it wasn't planned. Still brave," Prisca retorted.

"It's not brave if you do it instinctively. If you don't think about it, just respond impulsively," James argued back.

28

Jade had been listening, thoughtfully. "But what you do instinctively says something about who you are; what's in your heart. Take our good friend here, Drew: faced with a crisis that demanded quick action, he would pour everyone a glass of champagne."

A burst of laugher broke the tension of the half whispered conversation. The girls shook with giggles and Drew raised his glass to play the role, but pain flickered across his face, and for a moment his eyes fell.

Through the tittering and volley of witty responses no-one had noticed the cloud pass over his face, except Vanessa, who for a short time had been standing, unnoticed, in the cabin doorway, watching the whispered conversation. She saw the shadow pass over him and it troubled her. She gazed at his face, puzzling over the change, when suddenly his eyes lifted and for an instant opened into hers, washing her with uncertainty. She leapt out of view and hid in the dim-lit cabin, trembling. Her heart rushed wildly as she strained to hear the conversation. The jokes and laughter trailed off and they fell into a pause. Then she heard his voice speak into the silence. It was clearly his voice but altered somehow. And not whispered or hushed now, but as if he intended her to hear.

"What Jade said, some of what Jade said, is true. Your impulsive actions do reveal something about your heart; what your heart loves most, or who. Is it yourself, or someone else?"

"Well, he certainly didn't have much self-love, and he couldn't have been in love with Vee, unless he was a secret admirer. It still doesn't make sense," struggled Prisca.

"He had love in his heart, but it was the kind of love that made him willing to sacrifice himself for someone else's sake, even a stranger," Drew continued.

"I would like to be loved with that kind of love," said Prisca quietly.

"How is that different to the usual kind of love?" asked James, a little defensively.

"Because most people confuse loving with the desire to be loved." Drew's voice was surprisingly serious.

An uncomfortable silence spread through the group.

"What do you mean?" asked Prisca, labouring to regain a light tone.

Drew paused before he continued slowly.

"I just think that people often say they are 'in love' when what they're feeling really has more to do with themselves and satisfying their own needs. What they call 'love' is often a hunger for the pleasure someone can give them. Love should be more about caring for someone's good whatever that means for yourself." A hush fell over the group as Drew's voice tapered off.

Hidden in the cabin, Vanessa shook with agitation and surprise. Her cheeks burned violently as she struggled to continue the lunch preparations. Outside the silence continued awkwardly until Jade suddenly burst out indignantly.

"Well, that's good advice from Mr. Self Indulgence himself. If anyone has mastered self-gratification, it has to be our dear friend here."

Drew's face coloured and his voice faltered as he started to speak. "I just attempted to interpret love; I didn't claim to have experienced it. It's an idea of what love should be."

Vanessa found herself again drawn to the doorway, listening in disbelief.

Jade's tone was scorching. "How can you talk about love if you haven't experienced it? That is so absurd."

"Because I am not talking about my own experience." Drew struggled and looked uncomfortable. "It's a model of love, of being able to love unselfishly. Not for the pleasure it brings you but for what you can give to someone else."

Everyone had been staring at him with dumb faces through his awkward speech. James shook his head with a puzzled expression.

"You are the last person I expected to be having this conversation with. Your life exemplifies the opposite. Where do you get this model from?"

Drew squirmed. It suddenly seemed too hot, and he regretted his candid speech. He felt the sun beating against the back of his neck and sweat beading on his brow. He felt foolish and was dreading his next line.

"Well," he stalled, "it comes from observing the person of Jesus..."

"The person of Jesus!" Jade burst in vehemently. "I thought you hated Christians."

Drew stammered defensively. "I'm not talking about Christians; I'm talking about Jesus. If you'll let me explain." He took a breath slowly and looked away towards the horizon. "I just found it interesting once, to think about the person of Jesus and how he loved. He loved the unlovable, the ones other people despised. He loved his enemies who plotted against him. And he loved his friends after they deserted him. His great act of love was sacrificing himself to save everyone. He didn't love people because they were beautiful, he made them beautiful by loving them."

The boat rocked and the wind whipped around each figure as they sat in awkward silence, looking away to avoid catching anyone's eye.

It was Vanessa's voice that broke the silence, as she spoke from the cabin door, causing everyone to look around in embarrassment.

"It's beautiful. Isn't it what we all long for without knowing it." She continued with a puzzled tone. "But having discovered it, why do you go on living as if it isn't true? Why hasn't it changed you?"

"It takes effort to change. I like my dissipated ways." Drew raised his glass in a sad gesture.

"I don't think you like them at all." Vanessa's eyes were fixed on him with a new intensity. Drew looked away from the honesty of her face.

The tension was unbearable for Prisca, who began to fidget uncomfortably.

"I think we should eat that picnic you've been preparing."

She gave Vanessa a stern look, but Vee was deep in thought. Impatiently, she made her way across the deck, and manoeuvred Vanessa into the galley.

"I think we need to get food out there quickly," she muttered sharply. "It's all getting a bit strained."

Prisca bustled noisily, trying to scatter the serious mood with her energy and light comments. She took charge over Vanessa's half prepared lunch, and piled salad, cheeses, cold-cuts of meat, and crisp baguettes onto trays, carrying them briskly into the silent circle of friends.

The sun glowed in their tanned and smiling faces, glinting off sun-glass screened eyes. They met the arrival of the food with noises of appreciation. Vanessa sat limply down, feeling even more emptied and disturbed. She gazed vaguely at the sea as she heard the chatter and laughter of her friends swell like the distant surf and breaking of waves, their individual voices blending into a tumbling stream of words and opinions. She picked absently at the food, filling a roll with cheese and salad, without any real hunger to inspire her. Words drifted over her, as her thoughts remained trapped in her heavy emotions.

"Are you sure we don't have artichokes? I told you to bring artichokes. How can I enjoy a picnic without artichokes? I'm going to look for myself." Jade unfolded her nut- brown form and traipsed into the cabin with an air of assumed irritation. The conversation continued to bubble and ripple meaninglessly over Vanessa's brooding sense of unhappiness.

She lifted her eyes to sweep in her surroundings. Around her sprawled the trappings of a privileged and indulgent lifestyle, of good health and beauty, of sunshine and choice. Isn't this what everyone wants? she mused silently. The question pricked her growing sense of isolation. I should be happy, she thought. There are people who would envy what I have.

Jade sat down gloomily. "There are no artichokes."

Vanessa saw the hours stretching forward in empty futility and sighed heavily.

The moon trailed low over the dark ocean, sending a shimmering path of silver across its inky surface. The boat swayed and pulled at its anchor, as the currents heaved and tilted below with restrained power. The night air was still and warm.

The velvet sky was strewn with the glitter of white stars.

Chords of music wafted over the boat and mixed with the ringing sounds of laughter that danced briefly then disappeared into the stretching night.

Colour glowed in Vanessa's face as she leaned back laughing, her eyes flashing from face to face. She pushed her plate away. "I can't eat another thing."

"Then don't, my Lady. Dance instead." Drew's eyes washed over her, glad to see her happy again.

"Who's going to help me clean this up?" Prisca enquired as her eyes swept over the remains of their meal and searched each giggling face.

"No-one! Just leave it and stop spoiling the party," Jade implored impatiently.

The soft strains of music grew louder as Drew leant across to turn the CD player up. He stretched his arms out towards Vanessa.

"Dance. You look so beautiful when you dance."

Vanessa blushed and giggled as she searched her friends' faces. Jade shrugged gracefully.

"Please," Drew persisted.

"There isn't a lot of room for dancing," Vanessa observed.

"Not much, but enough. Am I enticing you?" Drew continued.

"No, but the music is," Vanessa laughed, as she swayed gently.

Drew took her arm and pulled her slowly to her feet. She turned lightly in his hands as he guided her.

"Are you happy again?" he breathed softly.

"On the outside," she smiled, as tears pricked against her eyes.

She twirled away from him, slipping out of his hold. Drew leant against the railing and watched as she floated in the music, turning gracefully in the tiny orb of light that bobbed over the black depths of the restless sea. In her dance she tried to slip away from the darkness that hovered ruthlessly around her, to inhale the silver beauty of the night, to hold the stars in her heart, and draw away from the searing heat within.

"May I have the pleasure of this dance?" James bowed mockingly as he invited Jade onto the floor.

"That is very kind of you, Sir," Jade crooned as she rose and joined James.

"What about me?" complained Prisca. "Who am I going to dance with?"

"You can dance with me," called Drew. "She doesn't seem to need a partner."

Laughing and tripping, they bumped against each other in the tiny deck space at the rear as the music tumbled through their wine-drenched minds.

Vanessa felt the hovering darkness press against her as she watched her friends fall stupidly about. An angst quivered in her heart as the warmth of the wine drained away.

As tears filled her throat, she backed away from the staggering, lurching dance. Emptiness opened like a cold grave within her, and she shrank from their flushed emotions.

The moonlight shone like a ribbon touching the bow. She tentatively lifted her trailing skirts, and placing one foot in front of the other, she stepped carefully down the narrow side of the boat, stretching out her slender arms for balance. The music churned its cheap melody that no longer lured her hungry heart.

"What are you doing?" a voice called anxiously.

"I'm balancing on a knife edge between the moon and the sea; between cold beauty and death."

Drew broke away from the clumsy dance.

"Come back, Vee. You're being stupid. You can't walk along there. You've had too much to drink, and it's dark."

The dark expanse of sky joined with the bottomless depths of the sea in a swallowing, enveloping fear.

"I am one pale strand of life, one frail flame trembling in the relentless reaches of time."

"Stop Vee!"

"I just want to sit in the light. See how the moonlight rests in a pool over there."

"Stay where you are. I'm coming."

Her face gleamed white like the moon as she tossed her waving curls over her shoulder and looked back. Her smile was stretched in sadness, her eyes heavy with despair. Her pale, outstretched arms waved like a ribbon in the wind as the boat suddenly rose and sank on the lurching swell of the sea. Her voice trailed in an alarm that was snatched up by the night breeze and scattered. The giddy dancers fell laughing against each other as the boat see-sawed. Drew was thrown against the side of the rocking boat as he watched her stagger and struggle for balance. He gasped as he saw her white form fall through the moonlight and sink into the darkness, swallowed up from sight by the enveloping sea.

Drew gripped the railing in anguish. Around him voices wailed in an irritating chord. People pushed against each other in purposeless panic as they rushed hopelessly about the boat. His eyes were fixed on the slight, bubbling pool of turbulence that glinted white in the consuming inky blackness. He clenched his hands, and sweat pierced his brow as he wrestled with himself.

Vanessa slid easily through the cold black expanse. There was a sudden icy shock then silent, blanketing darkness. She plunged through the depths, hugged by the blackness which spread out invisibly around her, sinking silently. She spread her arms out to stop her descent, and tried vainly to kick her legs, but found that they were trapped, bound tightly together in the tangled lengths of her skirt which had wound around her. She struggled and crawled with her arms as her lungs started to call for air. She rolled and writhed helplessly without any sense of direction. She tumbled through the darkness, blindly; desperation growing. Her chest screamed for air as she rolled and sank.

As dread and suffocation pressed against her, ghostly images swam out of the darkness and leered at her hauntingly; snap-shots of her life which glowed and tormented as the doors to her memory were wrenched away, and she saw all her thoughts, feelings and experiences parade about her in naked clarity.

A grey face with a bitter smile floated menacingly up to her, laughing coldly. She felt her mind recoil in horror, and crimson shame rage through her body.

"Hello. Remember me?"

"No. Who are you?" she asked fearfully.

"I am the men you loved briefly and then discarded. You danced your beauty before me, drank from my affections, and then spat me out."

"But I never meant to hurt you," she stammered nervously. "Each time I really hoped you where going to be 'the one'; I thought that I was really in-love, and there wouldn't be any others. But I was wrong. A mistake. That's all. I never meant to hurt your feelings."

"You wanted someone to make you happy, to take away your fears and loneliness; it was always about you. I could never be enough to satisfy you. So you took from me until you'd had enough, and then you left me."

"My affections changed. I changed. I'm sorry," she begged. "Forgive me." He was gone.

Around her chased four women, their hair streaming in matted strands, their voices screeching like crows as they argued ferociously. They stopped suddenly and turned to her.

"How dare you pretend to be my friend, and speak to her about the things I told you," they all shouted together in shrill, wailing voices. "I trusted your integrity, but I shouldn't have. You were talking behind my back the whole time."

"You're wrong, I wasn't speaking against you. I loved you. I was speaking in love about you, because I care about you," she reasoned desperately with flaming cheeks. "I was trying to help you, not harm you."

"You're trying to justify yourself," they spat in answer. "You loved talking about us; it was warm and deep like a hot bath, and thrilled your senses. Don't make excuses."

Vanessa shuddered as they swept away, and the desolate, grasping darkness dragged her further and further down.

A gaunt figure floated some distance away, hungrily feeding on cakes and sweets and all kinds of treats that she was hugging and hoarding to herself. Her thin body was bent and twisted, as she drifted alone in the vacuous darkness, mumbling vaguely to herself.

"Pamper yourself; you deserve it. You are always thinking of others, you can look after yourself for a change. If you indulge yourself, you will have more to give others. You need all these lovely things; don't feel guilty if others are hungry."

The gaunt figure stopped and looked up, startled. "I do care about others; I care about them immensely. There is just nothing I can do for them. I barely have enough for myself."

A glimmering ball of colour sped through the darkness, darting elusively. A shoal of figures rushed after it with outstretched arms, turning and chasing as it dived about in cascading light. Hope escalated in a thundering crescendo as hands nearly grasped the shimmering orb, but vanished suddenly as the ball disappeared with a puff.

Vanessa peered through the inky gloom which swarmed with unpleasant memories that filled her with fear and shame. She groped towards some transparent images which hovered in a thin, failing light. She studied them with a flickering sense of hope as a smile almost touched her lips. Expectation crept into her heart as she recognised that they were her achievements. She watched all her successes milling around; her jobs, her degree, her beautiful home, her abilities and good looks. She feasted on them, trying to fill the horrible emptiness that was growing inside her trembling self. But the more she examined them, the paler they grew until they seemed to fragment and vanish into the shifting sea. Her woe grew even deeper and more penetrating, filling her bones with dread, worming through her flesh.

With scorching clarity each lie, each unkind word, every depraved and selfish thought, every self-serving deed was vividly exposed and projected through the inky depths.

She huddled her naked heart as she sank deeper, seeing darkness and pain stretching eternally ahead in never-ending grey solitude.

"No," she whimpered. "No. I'm sorry. Please save me."

Something tugged her violently from behind. Something was thrashing painfully in the water, kicking, dragging; her clothes were pulling tightly around her neck. She was too weak to struggle against the pulling and jerking. The darkness had filled her mind, inertia had overcome her body. She drifted in a dark cloud as the splashing and struggling battled around her. Somewhere in the distance voices where shouting, and pain was pressing against her. She retched and spluttered as the pain and pushing increased.

"Stop", she moaned. "Stop hurting me."

Something hard, rough and cold pressed against the length of her body. She coughed and vomited in violent paroxysms. The greyness was growing thinner and sounds were growing louder. She prised her eyes open a little. She was lying on the deck. She could see feet and legs surrounding her in a circle, faces peering down. She slowly turned her head. Beside her was a heaving body spread out on the deck, gasping for breath. She struggled for recognition. It was Drew, his wet clothes clinging to him, his shoulders rising and falling as he struggled for air.

Wrapped in a blanket, she shivered and cried. Drew hugged her and smoothed her wet hair.

"It's O.K. You're safe now. It's all over. You're safe."

"No! You don't understand. It's not over. It's just started. Now I know I'm not safe. Before I thought I was, but now I know that I'm not."

"Shsh. Don't fret. James is motoring back to the marina. We'll take you home. You're fine."

Vee's tears broke in painful sobs.

"You've just had a fright. You'll be O.K. soon." Drew struggled to comfort her.

"But I'm not O.K," Vanessa struggled to say through shuddering tears. "I'm not O.K." Her voice shrank into a whisper. "I've just seen what I'm really like, and I know that I'm not O.K." Her back shook as the bewildered Drew tried to hug her to himself.

Warmth crept along her back as the sun rose in the sky. Blinking painfully she looked around. She slowly tried to move her body, stiff and painful from sleeping on the hard deck. She could see other bodies hugging into blankets and trying to keep the sun out of their eyes for a little longer. She whispered to Drew, "Are you awake?"

"What?" he mumbled.

"Are you awake?"

"Sort of."

"Thank you. Thank you for rescuing me."

He was silent.

"I mean it. Thank you for risking your own life to save me."

"It's O.K," he mumbled sleepily.

He turned gingerly over, his face grimacing as he moved his painful body. Vanessa was sitting cross-legged, alert and intense. He rubbed his stinging eyes, blinking in the bright morning sun. He looked at her face, lined with worry.

"You're thinking about last night. What did you mean about seeing yourself?" Drew asked awkwardly.

Vanessa's head dropped as the dark images flooded her raw memory.

"Well," she began. Her voice stumbled as she struggled to find a way of expressing the troubling thoughts that were eroding her peace. "This will sound awful, and I don't mean to be nasty." Her voice dropped to a whisper. "I like Jade and she is my friend, but I have always thought of myself as being quite different. She is sort of openly selfish and seductive, I suppose. She says exactly what she thinks; gets what she wants; steps on people, and makes no apologies. That's just her. Well I never thought I was perfect, I know I've made some stupid mistakes, and I am weak in many ways, but I did think I was better than her; more caring. Not completely selfish."

Vee's voice faltered as she struggled with her thoughts. "It was very strange last night. I saw things in the darkness. I saw that I'm really no better."

"But you are," Drew interjected with passion. "You are the sweetest person I know."

"That is kind of you, but I could just see my life as wasted rubbish. I've been living for the next exciting emotion, the next pleasant experience, the next achievement or success, the next pearl of hope to drop into my life and make it all beautiful. I might be kind or pleasant in the process, but underneath it all it's about me. I just cover it up better than Jade does. In a way she is the more honest person."

"I think you are being hard on yourself," Drew continued thoughtfully. "You have had a big fright and it's disturbed you. Once you get home, things will get back to normal and you will feel better about yourself."

"That is what disturbs me most; forgetting what I've seen and going on the same, living the same futile, selfish life. That is my pain. I feel guilty."

"What are you guilty of? You haven't murdered anyone. You're not guilty, just shaken up."

"But that's the point. I have always felt that I was O.K. because I hadn't done anything really bad. But I was always comparing myself with people that I saw as being worse than me, and seeing myself in the better light. Now I can see that all my life is essentially about me and my feelings and pleasures, and for some reason this doesn't seem right. Even when I'm doing things for other people, I'm doing it to justify my own life. It does make me feel guilty. It just seems a bit pointless."

Vanessa paused. She and Drew stared uncomfortably away from each other.

The silence continued painfully.

"I just don't know how to get rid of the feeling of guilt," she added eventually.

Drew's voice was quiet and tinged with shame. "Just suppress it; push it aside. It's easy. I've been doing it all my life. Drink, laugh, joke, play. Anything that works!"

Vee looked at him with surprise, feeling confused and dismayed. "Can you really go on forever like that?" she puzzled.

Drew shrugged dismissively and looked away.

"I'm sorry. It must sound like I'm not being very appreciative towards you, after you jumped in to save me," she mumbled awkwardly. "I do appreciate it."

The silence continued.

"Have I hurt your feelings?"

Drew's face contorted with unfamiliar emotions. "I guess last night I saw something about myself too." His voice shook and stopped. "I generally feel very little obligation to do good for others if it doesn't suit me." His voice broke off again. "But when I saw you disappear into the black sea, I knew I didn't want you to be gone forever. That I'd miss you too much. And I think too that I want some of that love that I was talking about." He turned his head away. "So I jumped in to get you back, but maybe you are already gone."

"What do you mean?"

"Well, if you are on a course of spiritual improvement, you certainly won't have time for reprobate characters like me."

Vanessa's head hung in blushing confusion. Everything seemed to be getting more complicated and uncomfortable. She couldn't understand Drew. She just wanted to be home now. Then she recalled that home was going to be messy too, and her heart ached with desperation.

She slid noiselessly into the hospital room, self-consciously hugging the wall and clutching a bunch of flowers in shaking hands. Her eyes clung to the floor as nurses bustled in and out of the door, their shoes squeaking on the linoleum, their trolleys rattling boldly. She slowly lifted her eyes and scanned the room. A high bed stood in the middle of the polished floor, crowded by a baffling array of metal frames and other equipment; tubes and slings of various kinds were draped and hung; pumps pulsed and sighed; white linen was spread in smooth, starched planes. She squirmed uncomfortably and lost sense of what she was doing.

"Hello."

The voice startled her and drew her eyes to the centre of the bed. Dark eyes smiled back. Embarrassment pricked her flushed cheeks.

The man continued to smile at her while she wrestled with the scene before her. Most of the young man's body seemed to be wrapped in bandages. His right leg was suspended by ropes and pulleys; one arm was in a sling; crimson blood snaked through a narrow tube into his left arm; more tubes protruded from his bruised chest. She shook with distress.

"Can I help you?" he continued.

"I just…" She coughed hard to clear her shaking voice. "I came to thank you."

She held out the flowers awkwardly. Her eyes fell and she added hurriedly, "I'm the one you pushed away, when the car came. So thank you," she mumbled timidly.

"I know who you are," he answered softly. "The flowers are lovely. Thank you!"

Vanessa looked around for somewhere to place the bouquet, but finding nowhere suitable continued to stand holding them.

She thought to enquire about how he was feeling but changed her mind. She cleared her throat again, struggling to know how to continue.

"I was just wondering…" Emotion filled her voice and she paused again. She continued in a broken whisper, "Why did you do it?" She blinked rapidly as tears flooded her eyes.

The man thought for a little while and formed his words carefully. "Well, I suppose I saw the car heading for you, and I could see that the only way to stop it hitting you was to step into your place and take the impact instead; so I did."

"But I don't know you," Vanessa exclaimed in amazement. "Why would you be injured in the place of someone you don't know? Why would you take my pain on yourself? You could have been killed."

"Someone was injured in my place when I didn't know Him, and he was killed. He died my death so that I can have his life. I used that life to save you from being hit by the car."

She continued to stare in disbelief, unsure of whether to say more, but her visions from the sea were hanging grimly in her mind.

"There is something else," she added hesitantly.

"Yes." His deep eyes smiled patiently.

"I had another disturbing experience yesterday. It's difficult to explain," she mumbled awkwardly.

"I fell into the sea, and I was drowning. I saw all sorts of ugly things; ghostly images floating about. Sort of pictures of my life, the things I had done and said. It was horrible and frightening, but worst of all, I feel guilty. Like I've done something wrong. My friends keep trying to convince me that I haven't and my guilt isn't real, but I know it is. Do you understand?"

The man watched her face as he waited to answer. "You have glimpsed death; where every deed, thought and word is judged, and rewarded without partiality." He shuddered as he spoke. "Who can stand in that judgement?"

Desperation rose in her heart as she felt the dread and agony of what she had seen.

"Is there no escape?" she asked miserably.

"Only if someone tastes this death for you; if someone takes your place and is judged instead of you."

"But is there anyone who would taste death in my place?"

"There is one who can. Only one."

She looked to him, baffled.

"Who?" she pressed.

"Someone who has existed for all time, and who has no wrong-doings of his own to be judged for; someone who has a perfect life to exchange with your marred one. Someone who has tasted death but has not been overcome by it; someone who has known you since before you were conceived, and loves you enough to suffer in your place; someone who rules in glory over life. It is him you must find and he will save you and take away your guilt."

"But how do I find him?"

The man pushed a heavy book towards her. "You'll find him in his word, if you seek him with all your heart."

Vanessa's eyes fell onto the open page.

"He was wounded for our short-comings and crushed for our wrong-doings, upon him was the punishment that brought us peace."

Vanessa's dark eyes glinted with tears. She looked up at the man. He nodded silently and smiled.

GLIMPSES

Of the Heart

Strokes of pale pink brushed the inky sky as morning crept over the horizon, silhouetting the man who knelt on the hilltop, bent in solitary prayer. As light opened up the day, he straightened himself and stood up, his eyes moving in a wide arc over the city of Jerusalem which sprawled untidily at his feet. His heart heavy, he followed the path that led him down the grassy slopes of the Mount of Olives, through the jostling city streets, to the foot of the temple. Pain burned deep in his throat and chest as he squinted up at the colossal monument of stone, gleaming in the bright morning sun. Throngs of men, burdened with pious obligations, streamed through the arching gates and spilled into the temple courts. Wrapping his thin cloak closer around his body, for the sun had not yet warmed the chilled air, he sighed heavily and joined the lines of men filing through the gates.

She stood in the open doorway of her house, gazing into the empty, half-lit street. A pink haze was creeping into the sky above her. She pulled her scanty shawl closer over her thin form and shivered in the cool morning breeze. Behind her gaped the empty house still gloomy with the morning's quarrel.

She thought back over the morning, still hardly begun. She had woken up with the first cock crow to find him gone. As she had reached across in the darkness to find his sleeping form, she had discovered only the emptiness of crumpled covers. Bewildered, she had rushed anxiously downstairs to find him shoving clothes into a bag.

"What are you doing?" she had cried in alarm.

"What does it look like I'm doing?" he had replied in annoyance.

"It looks like you're packing," she had answered, desperation creeping into her voice.

"Well, that's what I'm doing," he had snapped.

"But why are you packing?"

"Because I'm going away; why else would I be packing?" His brusque voice had been stretched with irritation.

"But you didn't tell me you had to go away again. You've only just got back."

"Something has suddenly cropped up. I can't help it. It's just business."

They had argued back and forth, she had cried, he had shouted. Then he had coldly left. She had lifted her arms to him.

"Say goodbye properly." He had walked by, his head turned away.

"Won't you even kiss me?" He had picked up his bag and thrown it roughly over his shoulder.

"When will you be back?" Her voice had trailed into the dark streets. She had watched his black figure glide past the shadowy houses.

She still stared into the streets as, little by little, the houses grew clearer and emerged from the night. The golden disc of sun peeped cautiously over the rooftops, then glazed the highest points in amber light. She blinked as a few glistening rays squeezed past the shadows and dazzled her tear-filled eyes.

Footsteps crunched nearby. Startled, she lowered her face and turned to go inside.

"Don't go. It's just me."

She looked up, surprised. A figure was walking towards her. She squinted into the growing sun to make out the face, but he was hidden in darkness.

"Who is it?" she asked uncertainly.

"It's me." Suddenly his face was very close and she could see it was her old friend.

"You shouldn't frighten me like that." She sniffed as she hurriedly tried to wipe her face on her shawl.

"You've been crying." His voice was tender with concern.

She darted away from his searching eyes, retreating into the house. A single candle cast a flickering sphere of light around the small room. In the fireplace glowed the last embers of a fading fire. She knelt on the hearth and sprinkled twigs over the coals, blowing gently to ignite them.

"Let me do that for you." Her friend stepped quickly across the room and grasping the bellows and a little straw, worked to raise a flame. The woman, noticing that the door still stood ajar, walked across to the open doorway. Light was now streaming into the streets. She leant out a little to inhale the fresh morning air, and as she did, almost bumped into one of her neighbours who was approaching along the footpath.

"Oh, hello. I didn't see you there."

"Apparently not," replied the passing woman in a huffy tone.

She stepped back to allow her neighbour to pass.

"Your husband had to leave again on business, I hear. Wasn't home long, was he!" Her voice was smouldering with curiosity.

The young wife's face clouded with humiliation, her eyes smarting with tears. Her friend's voice called her back.

"Anna, come away from the door."

"Oh, I see you have company," the neighbour crowed, her snake eyes peering into the room.

"Please excuse me," Anna stammered, and in great confusion and embarrassment, closed the door.

Shaking, Anna drew back a chair from the simple wooden table and sat down.

Her friend smiled up at her. Flames leapt from the hearth bathing the room in a golden light.

"You shouldn't be here, you know. She will try to cause all sorts of trouble for me." Anna's voice trembled.

"Silly old gossip. My dearest friend is distressed and I've come to comfort her."

His kind words burned in her heart and overflowed in hot rolling tears.

"Anna. You poor thing." He rose to his feet and stepped quietly to her side. Pulling a chair up, he sat down and grasped her hand. "Your fingers are so cold. Were you standing at that door for long?"

She made no reply but tears tumbled down her cheeks and her body convulsed softly.

His fingers gently stroked the back of her hand.

"Try to tell me." His voice was patient and low.

Anna whispered through her bubbling tears, "He's left again."

The chair legs screeched as the man jumped to his feet, pushing back the chair in agitation. He paced angrily before the fire, clenching his mouth in bitter emotion. He glared at the cowering form of Anna, her face hidden in her hands.

His voice broke from him in snatches of words as he struggled with all his might to control the torrent of emotion. "That man is a brute."

"You mustn't say that," Anna mumbled.

"Why must I not say that?" His voice rose like a wave ready to break. "It's the truth."

"He's my husband and I won't hear you speak disrespectfully of him."

The man stared at her, speechless, his rage frozen by her simple faithfulness. He stood silent as his feelings surged and tore at him.

His voice was soft again. "Your beauty is wasted on him."

Anna squirmed. "Don't."

He stepped up to her, and kneeling beside her he placed his finger over her lips to silence her. Bewildered, she looked into his face, the firelight dancing in her wide eyes.

"Is he your husband when it is me who has loved you since I was a boy and you were a girl?"

Her eyes drank in his face as his words burned in her heart. Slowly his hand fell from her mouth and lay despondently on the table, limp from the boldness of his revelation.

With her eyes still lingering over his face she quietly spoke. "We might love but I am promised to him."

"Your parents promised you to him." His voice shook with hurt.

"But I promised God to be his wife."

He leant his head forward until his forehead rested on hers, grief coursing through his body and mind. His words escaped like a whisper, as soft as a breath.

"I wish you had promised yourself to me."

Tears streamed down both their faces as they sat so close that she could feel his breath warm on her cheek. Anna's hands lay still cold in her lap as warm drops of tears fell and mingled in her palms. Hesitatingly she lifted her hands and placed them gently on either side of his face. She slowly tilted his face until his eyes met hers then with her heart pulsing she placed her lips on his.

The door burst open in a sudden, explosive moment that crashed through the room and jerked them apart. They turned baffled and afraid towards the door, dreading the next moment. Two figures stood large and dark in the doorway. Anna was flooded with shame and her hands nervously clutched her shawl to draw it closer, to cover her guilt. Her friend stood up and stepped boldly towards the door.

"What do you want?" he called.

One of the figures walked into the room, his large bulk filling the threshold.

"I want my wife, that's what. What do you think you're doing in here?"

"That's him, that's the one I saw. Goodness knows what would have happened if I had not made it my business to find you before it was too late." Anna heard the squawking voice of her neighbour as she pushed her way into the house as well.

"So, is this what goes on when I'm out of the house?" Anna's husband's ugly voice sneered accusingly.

"No, it is not," Anna and her friend both replied defensively. Anna looked across at her dear friend and spoke in the steadiest voice she could manage.

"You must go now and leave this to me."

He was trembling with pain. "No. I can't leave you with him."

"You must," she insisted forcefully. "I am his wife. Go."

Her eyes convinced him that she was
determined, so with a desperate last look at her he
edged towards the door. Her husband stepped
further into the room and allowed him to pass.
Anna's husband fixed his angry stare on his
trembling wife.

"You have dishonoured me."

"I'm sorry," she whispered. "I have betrayed
you and God. Forgive me."

"Forgive you!" he screamed. "Forgive you." He
stared at her in disgust. "We shall see what they
make of you at the temple."

She dropped her head and shuddered. Her mind
whirled with fear and shame. She felt him drag her
across the room and past the sneering woman who
was still loitering in the doorway. The bright sun
of the open street burned against her, exposing her
shame, as he dragged her through the throngs of
staring people, shouting, "My wife is an adulterer."

She felt the crowd growing and pressing around
her as her head swam, nauseous and dizzy. His
fingers were biting into the soft flesh of her upper
arm as he dragged her stumbling and faint up the
polished steps of the temple. She felt the eyes of
everyone turn against her in icy judgement. The
cold, marble floor struck her knees painfully as he
threw her onto the ground before the feet of the
scribes and Pharisees. She looked first at their clean
sandaled feet, then at the crisp hems of their white,

starched robes: then tilted her head up to meet their cold, uncaring eyes.

She dropped her head onto the ground and prayed. "Dear Lord God, forgive me for my sin. Have mercy on me."

The sun beat on the face of the young man who was seated in one corner of the temple court, teaching. Around him sat a crowd listening intently, straining forward in their eagerness to hear, their hearts burning with joy at the wonderful things he was saying, their eyes fixed on his face.

A little distance beyond this circle of listeners was a number of men, loosely gathered, who stood muttering to each other disapprovingly, picking fault with the young speaker.

"I think we've heard enough," sniggered one condescendingly. "Come, let's not waste any more time." With a proudly tilted head, he turned to move away.

"You go if you want, but I intend to stay and debate his heretical notions. What cheek to sit teaching in direct contradiction to the Pharisees! I'd like to teach him something."

"Oh!" the first speaker responded. "I can see you're quite worked up."

"I'm furious!"

Suddenly the young man's voice stopped. He looked past all the people and searched the temple court as if he was expecting someone. One by one the heads of his listeners turned around also, trying to discover what he was looking at.

"Can he see someone?" low voices mumbled inquisitively.

"I don't know. There are so many people here, how can he hope to find one person?"

Still the man paused from his teaching and looked expectantly, and still heads turned back and forth uncertainly.

Suddenly it became clear that a commotion was moving towards them through the crowd. Heads stretched and turned to glimpse what was happening. They could hear the whimpering cries of a woman and soon could see a small group of Pharisees and Scribes passing disdainfully through the people. Behind them walked a now rather frightened looking man, and a woman being half marched, half dragged by two guards.

As the group approached, the crowd parted to let them pass. One of the Pharisees approached the group of critical onlookers and spoke in a conspiratorial voice.

"I think we have the perfect opportunity to expose this young fraud. We shall trap him with a question."

They all nodded derisively.

Anna swayed as the heat beat against her and the dust filled her dry mouth. A crowd of people swarmed around her in a vague indistinct mass, pushing against her, hostile and jeering. She saw her husband's face, pale and anxious. His anger had carried him too far. She glimpsed her friend peering fretfully through the crowd. Her stomach retched with dread, her lips moved constantly in prayer.

A large oval face, lined with cold bitterness, jutted forcefully into hers, occluding the crowd. His eyes examined her with cruel expectation. She trembled as he grabbed her and shoved her roughly until she was standing before the whole crowd. She felt the whispers hissing and lashing as she stood exposed and disgraced. The faces swam as tears blurred her sight and her head reeled.

A pious voice rang above the murmur of the crowd, clear and resounding.

"Teacher, this woman was caught in the act of adultery. In the Law, Moses commanded us to stone such a woman. Now what do you say?" His eyes slid sideways to catch the grim, satisfied smile of his friends.

Anna's eyes searched wildly for the teacher to whom the question had been addressed. She was surprised when a young man who had been sitting on the ground, amongst the people, stood and turned towards her. Her eyes fell on him. He didn't look like the other teachers; he was dressed in simple country clothes. His eyes were open and deep, and searched her with a penetrating gaze which exposed her heart, filling her with fear and joy. She stood fixed by his face unable to see or hear anything but him. Her eyes followed him as he bent down and began to write on the ground with his finger. The Pharisees looked at each other in vexation.

"How do you answer us, Teacher?"

Still the man continued to write on the ground. Again and again they questioned him. Anna watched with wonder as he calmly proceeded despite the frustration of the Pharisees.

Finally he stood up and looked them all in the face.

"If any one of you is without sin, let him be the first to throw a stone at her." Then he bent down and continued to write on the ground.

An oppressive silence stilled the crowd. Red-faced men fidgeted uncomfortably while the man quietly wrote. One by one, some of the older men shifted awkwardly away. The man continued to write and did not look up. More and more men slid uncomfortably away, heat glowing in their faces.

Eventually the man stopped and looked up. Only he and the woman were left. She trembled as she searched his face.

"Where are they?" the man shrugged. "Has no-one condemned you?"

"No-one, sir," she said.

"Then neither do I condemn you. Go and sin no more."

Of His Face.

A stream of yellow light and bursts of laughter, spilled out onto the street. Kate stood awkwardly on the pavement, glancing nervously at the people filing past her. She dropped her eyes as another group of couples sauntered towards the entrance; women leaning elegantly on the arms of their partners, clicking in high heels, swishing in long silk dresses; tiny satin bags swinging on their slender wrists. The men breathed smooth confidence in black suits and bowties; shoes snapping up the steps as they glided through the open door into the Art Gallery.

Kate squirmed as heat crept into her cheeks, and she searched anxiously along the street for Merilee.

"Where is she?" her thoughts drummed impatiently. "She's always late." Nausea gripped her stomach.

The night was broken again by shuffling footsteps and giggles as more voices sounded from the dark street. Her eyes ran quickly over the reeling huddle of young people as they appeared out of the shadows, singing and see-sawing in a staggering mass towards her. Kate's eyes widened at the strange ensemble. They were a giddy collection of purple velvet and rustling black silk; of arching feathers and tottering shoes;

of everything outrageous and impractical. With difficulty they steered their course towards the door and manoeuvred unsteadily up the stairs, greeting the guests with a discordant ring of cheers.

Kate peered through the large windows into the brightly lit room and glimpsed fragments of the paintings between the glossy heads and vibrant dresses which milled and chatted with a deliberate air of extravagance, glinting with wine glasses and bubbling with a light froth of flattery.

Her eyes returned to roaming the street. Cars rolled slowly past with humming engines; the traffic lights flickered from red to green; voices shouted in the distance.

A tap on the shoulder startled her and she swung around.

"Merilee!"

"Hi," her friend sung lightly, her unnaturally crimson lips stretching into an exaggerated smile.

Kate's forehead folded into a frown as she surveyed the untidy bob of bleached hair streaked with peacock-blue, and the eyes gazing at her from under heavy lashes.

"Don't tell me off. I know I'm late," Merilee cut in. "Sorry," she pleaded in a sugary voice.

The hurt in Kate's face melted away and a smile crept into the corners of her mouth.

"You look fabulous," Kate mumbled, admiring the bold juxtaposition of colours and textures which hung elegantly on Merilee. She felt herself wilt in pale comparison, looking uncomfortably down at her own plain skirt and jacket.

"I don't think I can go in," Kate admitted shamefully.

"Why on earth not?" gasped Merilee. "It will be wonderful. We are so lucky to be invited," she continued happily.

"I don't know how to talk to these people," Kate whimpered.

"You don't need to say anything sensible," Merilee reassured her breezily. "Just smile and giggle a little. You'll be fine."

Merilee grasped her friend's arm and sailed towards the doorway. Kate contracted in a painful spasm of shyness, shrinking as she stepped into the room filled with vibrant people chatting and laughing. Merilee stretched and purred as admiring eyes turned towards her, showering her with praise. Kate froze with apprehension as she watched her friend glide into the throng, gushing with saccharin affection, cooing with wisps of clever conversation.

Merilee was the glowing nucleus of the party as she batted her glistening eyes and drank in compliments, swirling them like the scarlet wine she sipped from a glass.

Kate crept invisibly away from the doorway, inching towards the periphery of the room. She gingerly picked up an exhibition catalogue from a

pile and absorbed herself in studying it. With her
back turned to the party, she crawled slowly
around the walls, examining each piece of art, her
eyes jumping from catalogue to wall as she tried
to comprehend each artist.

Dark forms assaulted her mind as decay and
decadence was splashed in all its naked ruin
across the ragged sheets of canvas. Something of
their heavy despair settled in her fragile heart
like a pressing darkness.

A hand pulled against her averted shoulder.

"What are you doing?" Merilee interrupted.
"You're missing the party."

"I'm fine," Kate mumbled absently. "Do you
know these artists? This work is so disturbing."

"They are a bit weird, some of them," Merilee
admitted, screwing her face up in distaste. "But
they're not all like these," she assured her,
glancing around the gallery.

Kate continued to work her way around the
exhibition, mumbling brief words of apology as
giddy guests bumped absently into her. She
glanced around at the room which murmured
with mingled voices, some words ringing in shrill
distinction above the chatter; deep laughter
rumbling below. Heat pressed against her.

A large picture, framed in a simple rectangle
of gold, caught her attention. She inched her way
through the restlessly moving crowd till she
could see it clearly. A forget-me-not sky sailed

over apple-green hills, shimmering like sunshine. She drank in the rich colours and the illusion of summer. Her eyes moved to the foreground. Two women draped in white cloth, hugged each other in grief as they convulsed with tears, crumpled beside a coffin. The third figure was a man, also bent over in tears, one hand covering his distorted face while the other reached out to the women in a gesture of compassion and shared grief. Kate gazed at the crouching man, marvelling at the realism of the artwork; his dark hair falling in waves around his face and brushing his shoulders, the muscles of his strong arm rippling under his smooth olive skin; the folds of his white linen tunic gleaming in the sunlight; his bare feet planted firmly in the ochre dust of the dry ground.

With a burning heart, she searched the catalogue.

"He Bears Our Grief," by Jason Henry.

"Who bears our grief?" she demanded. The catalogue was silent.

She moved to the next similarly gilt-framed painting. She gasped as she immediately recognised the same idyllic background, the same baked foreground, the same man stretching out his arm. This time he was standing, turned away from her as he reached out to touch another figure standing close by. Kate recoiled in disgust as her eyes moved over a figure horribly deformed by disease, his clothes unrecognisable rags, his stature tortured by suffering. She followed the first man's arm as it reached out to this figure of misery and rejection, seeing his hand so gently grip and lift the stooped shoulder. Tears trembled dangerously in her quivering heart as her eyes dropped down to the catalogue.

"He Heals the Broken-Hearted," by Jason Henry.

"Same artist! Who is he?" she mused.

Another gold frame stretched out against the smooth white wall. She looked longingly for the man. She saw a cluster of a dozen men with wild bearded faces and rough tunics, gleaming in the dull lantern light that lit the dark room. They seemed to be just entering the room, some smiling at each other in conversation, some looking about the dimly lit chamber, some taking a seat on the cushions that circled a low table, others looking down at the figure that knelt on the hard, stone floor. Kate's eyes were drawn to this last figure. His tunic cast aside, he was kneeling with just a strip of cloth tied around his waist, his back bent in labour. She looked more closely. On the floor in front of him was a bowl of water and he seemed to be washing one of the men's feet. Perplexed, she looked up at the face of the man who was being washed. Tears were flowing down his rough face, his empty hands lying helplessly on his lap.

Again Kate turned to the catalogue for more information.

"He Came to Serve," by Jason Henry.

"Who *is* this Jason Henry?" she wondered with a burning heart. She looked up at the painting again. "He can certainly paint," she acknowledged, looking at the figures which seemed to almost step out of the canvas.

She glanced over the series of paintings again. "He seems to know something; to understand something beautiful, but I don't know what it is." Her eyes lingered on the man that appeared in all the paintings, with longing.

Kate glanced up as a thin man with dark hair caught her eye and smiled hesitantly. He was standing stiffly in a starched white shirt and black trousers, a short distance from her. Kate's eyes glanced from side to side, searching. "Is he smiling at me?" she wondered. Her uncertain lips parted in a hint of a smile.

The man stepped towards her. "Are you enjoying the exhibition?"

Kate wrestled for an answer. "I love these ones," she admitted enthusiastically, glancing up at the works. He continued to smile at her as she fumbled for more words. "I guess I don't really understand most of them," she admitted, unable to find any clever comments to make about the majority of bewildering images.

"And do you understand these ones?" the man continued quietly.

Kate groaned inwardly at her ignorance. Her eyes scanned for Merilee. "She knows how to talk about art," she thought desperately.

"Umm," she struggled, her face infused with distress.

"Just say what you think," the man encouraged her kindly.

Kate's words poured out in a rushing stream. "The colours attracted me first like a world more beautiful than this one, more real than reality. But it's the man who really fascinates me. He is so strong and yet so gentle. I find my heart longing to know him."

She drew in a long breath and looked to the ground, her cheeks flushed with her candid confession.

The man continued to smile. "Can I get you something to drink," he enquired politely.

"I don't drink," she mumbled apologetically. Her desperate lack of sophistication and glamour filled her with shame as she stood awkwardly.

"You must drink something," the man pressed with a good natured laugh. "Juice? Water? A cup of tea?"

"Oh," Kate mumbled, even more embarrassed. She caught sight of the round tray he was holding at his side. "He's the waiter. How stupid of me," she thought, trembling at her own mistake.

"I'd love a cup of tea."

"Milk? Sugar?"

"Just milk, thank you." She smiled as he glided away, watching him weave through the guests as he accepted empty glasses on his tray. She cast a searching look over the party and spotted Merilee migrating around the gallery, her voice ringing with sentimental greetings; "Oh, I haven't seen you for so long. How are you?" Her arms were outstretched in an embrace of wine-drenched emotion; her cheek lifted to receive the pecking kisses.

The man had just returned, placing a warm cup in her hand, when a disruption broke out somewhere near the door, shock rippling through the crowd in a wave of gasps and turned heads. The man excused himself and passed swiftly through the people. Kate's eyes followed in his wake, and glimpsed the intruder who was the cause of the outrage, standing with his head hanging in the doorway. Grasped on either side by two men who swayed as they struggled against their own unsteadiness, was a dishevelled looking man dressed in layers of filthy clothes, looking fearfully up through strands of long, dirty hair. He winced as streams of abuse were hurled at him.

"Go away. You won't get a drink here."

"You've probably had enough any way."

Kate watched the waiter approach him decisively, gripping him by the upper arm. She was surprised to hear his voice sounding over the din of derisive words and tittering jokes.

"It's alright, he's my friend. I invited him."

An awkward silence spread over the party as the waiter lead his friend into the gallery and served him from the buffet while the ruffled guests moved indignantly away.

Kate shrugged and moved on to the last painting in the series. Curiosity was tugging at her heart: who is Jason Henry? She looked at the various people filling the room and tried to guess. She watched a tall man waving his arms in animation as he entertained a huddle of giggling young women with admiring eyes.

"No," she thought. "Not him."

She saw a solitary man leaning against the wall looking quite ill, men staring at the paintings, men helping themselves to more wine, men bent in private conversations, the waiter smiling and chatting as he wove through the guests, serving. She had no idea who he was.

She drew her breath in sharply as she looked up at the last painting. The sun was setting in a red blaze over the curve of the hill; the lilac sky had turned to black. Three crosses stood silhouetted on the hill. She searched for the man. A pale figure lay bleeding on the ground at the foot of the cross, surrounded by a ring of weeping figures; the men he had washed, the ill he had healed, the mourners he had comforted, the outcasts he had embraced.

Kate blinked back the salty tears as her heart surged uncertainly. She lowered her swimming eyes to the catalogue: "Our Death He Died."

The night was black and cold as Kate and Merilee stepped out into the street.

"Did you have a good time?" Kate asked, her arm shooting out to steady Merilee who stumbled precariously.

"Wonderful time," she slurred. "I met so many interesting people. How about you? Did you meet anyone nice?"

Kate laughed. "The only person who chatted with me was the waiter."

"The waiter?" Merilee questioned. "Which one was he?"

"You know. He brought me a cup of tea and for some reason invited that funny looking man off the street."

"That wasn't a waiter," Merilee snorted. "That was the artist: Jason Henry. I thought you knew."

"For Christ also suffered once for sins, the righteous for the unrighteous, that he might bring us to God."

1 Peter 3:18

GLIMPSES

Of Another

Dark passages twist and maze as I claw my way through a labyrinth of gloomy, narrow streets; feet smacking against the ringing pavement as I suck air into my screaming chest. Panic clashes through my rushing head; numbing, blinding. I am stumbling, fleeing desperately, fighting through the darkness ahead; trying to outrun the horror that lurks behind, chasing and pursuing, almost grasping.

The darkness suddenly explodes with light. I stumble, blinking into the dazzle of sunlight; falling dizzily into the space of the plaza, reeling against the sudden expanse. The spreading pavement see-saws in nauseous waves; and oscillates with a haze of figures that swarm around me. A cold chill cuts through the sunlight. I shiver; sweat pricks my brow. My chest is still fighting for breath; my heart pounding noisily.

My feet are suddenly lead; soldered to the ground. I stand, panting; eyes scanning nervously, nausea pressing in violent waves. I steady myself against the lurching pavement, glancing anxiously behind and furtively ahead.

The swimming figures slide into focus and people emerge from the haze; people going about their business, oblivious, unsuspecting. People stroll unhurriedly, ambling between the market stalls. Fruit-sellers call in ringing tones; flowers wave their bobbing heads in masses of shimmering colour. The sunlight dances playfully over the fresh morning scene as pigeons peck and coo in a shifting mob.

I remain frozen; unmoving, anchored. Dread clings like a cold shadow, separating me from the day. I force my leaden feet forward. They step shakily across the paving stones, moving me awkwardly, self-consciously into the midst of the market. I move silently through the happy, jostling crowd; head still spinning, feet still unsteady, eyes clinging to the ground.

I slowly leave the crowd and make my uneasy way into the fringe of one of the pavement cafés that sprawl around the edges of the market square. I sink slowly into the curves of a chair and rest wearily, uncertain of the sunshine that hums with chatter and rings with street calls, and stare at the white disc of tabletop in front of me. Blood beats through my ears in hammer blows. The café and market slide unsteadily into the muffled distance.

A voice in a nagging monotone drives through my thoughts in growing intensity and suddenly startles me. An icy rush of fear courses through me, drawing blood from my swimming head. I turn to look up into the concrete face of a man.

"Is Sir ready to order?"

"Ready to order?" I stammer in bleating repetition. I struggle to bring my mind into focus.

"Yes, ready to order." Silence.

"Well!" the waiter sighs, in barely concealed impatience.

"A coffee, thank you. That's all."

He leaves with a brisk turn and I stare blankly for some time until I'm interrupted by the clink of china as a steaming cup is pushed into my gaze. I watch the steam curl upwards and drift away, and suddenly feel very cold. I wrap my fingers around the scalding cup and sip, shivering, huddling into the bowl of warmth.

I glance cautiously around me; my hesitant eyes scanning the spread of tables, the clusters of faces. The coffee spreads in warm waves, melting the chill and silence. Sounds trickle back into my hearing; voices carried on the light breeze are tossed about my ears. I feel the sun as it stretches lazily across my upturned face, and my breath catches the warm scents of spring.

I look sideways. Cigarette smoke trails between scarlet lips and strains of laughter as finger nails glint and rings flash in the morning rays. Tinted heads lean together, smug in their gossipy embrace. Grey suits and silk blouses rustle behind folded newspapers. The waiter roams wearily from table to table.

A comfortable thought settles in my mind and stirs a silly giggle deep in my belly. A smile pulls foolishly against my face. My features twitch with stifled emotions that heave and jostle silently within me. I ease into my anonymity and smirk inwardly.

I am cloistered by eyes all immersed in their gossip and journals, and nobody knows what I've done. The sun's bright light has bleached my shadowy deed. I stretch my legs and bask in the warmth, my guilt completely hidden and unseen.

The sun creeps across the sky, shifting shadows and baking the paving stones.

My thoughts start to drift with the drumming heat and lulling voices, as laughter washes and floats in musical waves. I rock and bob on the waves, my eyelids pressed closed by the white heat. Strains of conversation wind themselves into the drowsy thoughts that tumble about my mind. Each breath grows long and sweet as it gently rocks me.

Children's voices ring in singing games as they taunt and patter; their skipping feet beating a dance that chases my dreams. I struggle to smile, but my face has grown too heavy to move. The singing grows to fill the dark expanse of my mind.

"Johnny had a gun and the gun was loaded,
Johnny pulled the trigger and the gun exploded."

My eyes burst open as I am jerked violently awake, spluttering for breath. Dread presses in a crushing weight against my chest as I struggle for air. The children race and scatter, disappearing into the market throng. Shaking and pale, I turn my sick eyes from side to side. A shield of newspapers stands dispassionate and erect. My heart thumps noisily into the stretching, silent pause; blood screaming through my mind.

OF ANOTHER

I hear the clink of a cup settling into its saucer. Sweat steams at my forehead and collar, my shirt clings oppressively. Is someone watching me?

A businessman coughs and checks his watch. Glancing around, he turns the page of his paper and continues reading.

A young woman stands up, pushing her chair back noisily as she laughs and engages her companion in flirtatious chatter. She disappears suddenly into the square but returns abruptly after a minute, carelessly flinging a posy of flowers onto the table. Giggling she drops into her seat.

The waiter rests his tray on a table while he piles it with empty cups and a dirty ashtray. He wipes the table over with a cloth and heaves the laden tray towards the door. Conversations weave through each other in low, undulating tones. My breath grows easier. I wipe my damp neck with a handkerchief. It's hot now.

I signal to the waiter for another coffee. I'm not ready to move yet. I notice my fingers drumming the table nervously and withdraw them quickly onto my lap. The coffee arrives and I drink it in short agitated sips.

The cup is quickly emptied. My restless fingers grasp the spoon and poke it distractedly into the bowl of sugar, shovelling the white grains into conical mounds. I sigh and drop the spoon with a clatter into the saucer. I stretch back into the white glare of the sun which burns against my closed eyes.

I listen to the soft flapping of newspapers as the breeze flicks and tugs at the screen of printed sheets. Feet shuffle and chairs scrape in a distant, hollow rumble. My chest rises and falls with even breaths of warm air.

Cigarette smoke drifts across my face in an acrid, nauseous wave, stinging my nostrils. I sit forward blinking and looking around. In one unanimous, noiseless second the screen of newspapers is swept aside. A ring of eyes, black and staring, encircles me. In a sudden scrambling fit of knocks and shrieks and gripping pain, I find the world spinning recklessly, chairs sliding and crashing around me, my face wedged against the hard, cobbled ground.

I struggle desperately to draw air into my aching, winded chest. A sharp pain sears through my spine as the weight of a man pins me prostrate and helpless to the ground. Warm blood trickles from my mouth and collects in a salty, sickening pool. Horror spreads in a wave of frightened wailing as the crowd rushes, stumbling and frantic, away from me. I strain my eyes up from the stony pavement that presses against my cheek. Polished shoes take shattering steps towards me. A dark figure bends across my limited view, and I watch the shiny, hollow barrel of a gun grow large as it moves steadily towards me. In an instant the gentle sunlight is snatched away and I tumble into the inky, formless shadow that stretches across my mind.

I wait in the darkness, thrumming with discordant thoughts that jostle in an anxious throng. Footsteps snap sharply along the corridor and disappear into the muffled hum of voices that murmur somewhere beyond my door. I lay on the strange, hard bed staring wide-eyed into the darkness, finding no form or object to fix on, just inky blackness. Dread expands, heavy and suffocating, inside me; a clenched fist driving up through my stomach.

I sit up, fighting back sickness and bile, gasping for air. My bed starts to see-saw as I lose all my bearings. All I can feel is the stiff mattress beneath me. I grasp blindly for the wall beside me. My hand strikes its rough, cold surface and recoils abruptly, shrinking away from the hostile contact. I curl up, hugging my knees to my chest, wrapping my arms around myself, with a vague, intangible sense of longing for something lost; something warm and precious that I had but lost. Painful tears convulse me as I rock back and forth. A low wail resonates from my deepest part. What have I done? What have I done?

I lie suspended in the enveloping darkness that stretches endlessly around me. A haunted face meets mine, gleaming sickly with the pallor of death and fear. Red lips taunt and enrage me, and I hurl myself, beating and screaming, at the luminous face and the darkness, tearing it from my tormented conscience. My pain grips me in violent convulsions of remorse; I slam my head against the cold stone wall, again and again, trying to drive away the unbearable anguish, longing not to think or feel.

"Go away!" I scream into the darkness. I scream until my throat is dry and burning. I collapse, exhausted and heaving. I want to sob and say, "I'm sorry, I wish I hadn't done it!" but who is there to tell? What difference can it make now? It's done. It's done.

Sometimes through the tormenting darkness floats a perfect blue sky and it hovers over me, soaking me in the warmth of the midday sun. And I lift my face to the sun and smile. For a moment my smile seems to spread like warm sunshine right through my cold, empty body, and the agony melts away. I search through the shadow, straining wearily against the heavy burden of time, and I glimpse two children playing in a garden full of summer and the scent of lavender. Their father leans back on a garden bench, watching them with deep, shining eyes.

The boy snaps with an outburst of anger, and pushes his sister to the ground. She falls back, looking up at him with a face streaked with hurt and surprise. Her china doll flies from her hand and is smashed into pieces on the stone path. Father rushes over, sweeping my sister up in his wonderful, reaching arms. He catches my elbow as

I turn stubbornly away. His eyes hold me with his deep, knowing look. He wants me to say that I'm sorry.

"But I'm not sorry," I scream. "I'm not sorry." I am burning with rage.

His face is calm but determined, fixed with steadfast resolution. He sends me inside, stamping into the gloomy house, into the cold shadows, away from the sun. The gloom gathers and hangs on me.

Their voices are like distant, trailing songs, drifting away on the summer breeze, their laughter dancing lightly across the spreading lawn, entwined like ribbons sailing in the wind.

Tears swell in my aching throat and gnaw my sick stomach.

They are laced and bound together by golden threads of happiness that wind so easily around them.

I am cold and separate, hugging my isolation. I hear my sister's voice calling to me; the pieces of her doll are scattered across my memory, pricking my shame. My cheeks burn with a low heat as tears sting and convulse. I tremble with painful recollection.

"Why did I do it?" I shake and gnaw at my childish fingers. "It's done and I can't make it better."

I rush, sobbing, into the sun. My father turns with a quiet smile radiating from his strong face. He catches me in his arms, surrounding me, pressing me close. His hands smooth my hair and wipe away my tears.

"I'm sorry," I stammer; small words squeezed from my tight throat and quivering lips.

"I know," he smiles. "I know."

I rest in the warm glow of his words, and the gentleness of his face, his deep eyes caressing me through the darkness of my cell. Time lingers and my dream grows cold. I hug my rough blanket against the chill and the darkness stretches on.

White light, glaring harshly, slashes the velvet darkness that has become my consolation. I clutch my hands to my head, to cover my raw eyes, to blinker the stabbing brightness that pierces my head like a scream. I shrink away from the searching strip of light, huddling, pressing myself into the vanishing darkness; the bewildering darkness that has become my companion and comfort.

A shadow steps into the bright path of light that cuts across the floor of my cell. I look through squinting eyes at a figure standing in the open doorway. His eyes are resting on me; washing me in waves of familiarity, penetrating my secret thoughts. I am bewildered by the sure sense of knowing and being known.

I am small and young, giggling as I'm tucked into bed. I am red-faced and ashamed as I meet his seeing eyes. He knows. He sees what I've hidden in the shadows and brings it into the light. I can't lie to him. He is everything I need and everything I hate.

His voice rolls across me like a childhood dream. "Is there anything you want to say?"

"No!" I scream. "Go away; just go away."

"I'm here, you know. Always here. I love you."

The narrow path of light shrinks away from me as the door slowly closes. I am left in my darkness, my silence. I quiver with agitation; shaking, jittering. Tears sting my eyes. The darkness is all torn into fragments; my shady peace fractured. I am all friction and turmoil; my thoughts and pulse strum nervously.

He shouldn't have done this. He should have left me alone. I know what he wants, but he should have left me alone. My thoughts churn and repeat, revolving restlessly. He should have left me alone.

I search desperately through the darkness for my place of comfort, where I am so far from myself that I can't hear my screaming thoughts or feel my splintered heart.

Footsteps approach in crisp tones. The door squeaks and scrapes as it is dragged open. I am ready this time. I brace myself for the light as it pours through the widening gap. I cover my face with one arm and step forward.

A voice barks officiously.

"Well, come on then. Don't take all day."

I walk unsteadily through the doorway, into the brightly lit passage, shrinking in the blanching light, carrying my darkness like a shawl.

"Have to put these on, I'm afraid."

I shiver as they close the steel cuffs around my wrists and ankles, turning the key with a dreadful finality, and begin the slow, awkward shuffle along the glaring corridor that stretches narrow and straight, dragging my tethered feet across the polished linoleum that squeaks under rubber soles. Fear runs and screams in an electric frenzy, coursing through my body as it moves dumbly, heavily forward. Sweat drips and steams, soaking through my clinging shirt, crawling in stinging, salty streams that trail through strands of hair across my brow. My footsteps are dull and distant thuds, echoing in the lost extremities of the endless corridor. Alarm rings like a shrill monotone, filling my head and ears, cutting me off from the disappearing sounds around me.

Can anyone save me now?

My stomach is a sick and bilious knot, as I step numb and vacant towards a dreadful certainty.

Faces stare at me as I shuffle reluctantly into the dock; pale discs that dot the dark, wavering rows that encircle me in concentric, enclosing rings. Eyes scrutinise, paring my stubborn flesh.

I stare at my hands as they lay, limp and still, on my lap. I notice that they are just like my father's;

my hands are just like his. I see my father's hands reaching out to me; smooth, strong hands grasping me, drawing me near. A blade presses against my icy heart with painful longing. I shake the memory from my mind.

Hushed coughs and hoarse whispers splutter into the quiet pause that blankets the courtroom, smothering voices, stilling motion. My whirling mind is drawn into the ebbing stillness and my thoughts turn in slower and slower circles until they fall into a vacant stupor. The stifled murmurs around me drift further and further away as I slip deeper into my rigid, impassive stare.

I'm dimly aware of something tapping against my shoulder; rapid and vaguely annoying. I'm suddenly startled by a sharp pain in my side. I turn to find the guard poking me roughly.

"Stand up," he whispers crossly. I gaze absently around the room, a little surprised to find everyone standing. Their faces are a fixed wall of opposition, of heavy brows and indignation.

They don't like me.

I climb slowly to my feet and lean against the polished wooden rail that I find in front of me. I am bowed and bent over by a great exhaustion that presses and weighs down on me. I am too tired to care any more. Somewhere in the room it has all started. Official voices trumpet about, something is read aloud, something acknowledged. Everyone sits abruptly. Relieved, I sink back into my chair.

"Not you," a hiss snaps curtly from behind. I lift myself wearily and wait. More voices, more reading, a declaration. Typewriters tap sharply. Again that harsh, whispering voice behind, prompting. Everyone is still and silent, poised. The typists wait with suspended fingers, expectantly.

"How do you plead?"

I stare blankly into the waiting room. I shudder and feel the cold hand of death pass close to me. Every face is fixed on mine but I don't see them anymore. I swallow hard against nauseous revulsion, and with a steel voice and flint eyes, I reply, "Not guilty."

The room spins wildly around me. I grasp the rail with white hands, gripping intensely. The reeling motion slowly subsides, the sickness eases. The faces are still fixed and staring. The typewriters beat noisily. The pause continues. A single, clear voice breaks into the silence like a perfect musical note, ringing above the blurred cloud of faces.

"You may sit down now."

Recognition slams against me in cold, violent waves of shock. I slump down in my chair, weak and faint. I feel his eyes resting intently on me, and I look up. I stagger at the realisation. Is it really him? I am sick and shaking, my thoughts are in pieces. I can't hide; he knows. His face is grey and worn with disappointment, and I can see my lie bruising him with crushing blows. I am confused and shaken. I wish it didn't have to involve him.

He doesn't need to be hurt more. What a painful and absurd irony; my own father to be judge at my trial for murder.

I stand wearily, with sinking expectation. For days the arguing voices have volleyed back and forth, lathered in emotion; deep, expanded voices inflated with ringing persuasion. They batter about my ears like clanging, empty sounds that chafe and irritate my dull nerves. My days and nights have stretched in a long, flat monotone of voices and procedures, continuing slowly and steadily under the same glaring lights, broken by the same pauses and interjections, met by the same ring of staring faces. They ask me questions. I hear my answers spill into the hushed room; remote, dispassionate. Is that really my voice? I puzzle; it sounds so unfamiliar, so disinterested.

I watch the members of the jury file back into the courtroom carrying a solemn burden on their hanging faces, their eyes shifting and avoiding mine. They shuffle hastily into their seats. They have all condemned me and they feel guilty. I almost laugh. I shake with the absurdity of it. I examine each face as it assumes a false appearance of invisibility and calm. I see each man struggling with his own conscience, with the heavy responsibility he has. I stare as each one is forced to the agonising point of committal. A voice passes like a wave from face to face, rippling into the still of the room, a slow repeating tone, a reverberating echoing, "Guilty."

The faces swim and blur in a nauseous cloud. I slump back into my chair, dazed.

"The court will adjourn until tomorrow for sentencing." The gavel falls with an echoing blow. "All rise."

Eyes follow me with a look of horror and realisation as they pull me roughly to my feet and lead me out of the side door. There is no more compassion for the guilty. Their curiosity is gone and they recoil from me.

Back in my cell, the darkness encloses me like a tomb. I am in the deep, impenetrable blackness of the eternal night. The air is close and suffocating and full of the screaming dead. Reality jars my mind with its rigid and steel-like finality. My whole grasp of the future is uprooted and overturned. I am lost, hanging in a cold, enveloping dread, suspended between life and death, my thoughts caught in a turning wheel of despair.

The opening of the cell door grates distantly in my ears. A dark figure creeps pensively in and crouches in the shadows. I am only dimly aware of his waiting form and sighing breath.

"They hang murderers, you know." His voice jolts me like a screaming alarm. My skin retracts in an icy shiver.

"Look at me." His voice beckons with all the deep tremors of his love, so strong and yet so gentle.

I flare and ripple with irritation. My mouth bursts with a stream of curses and ugly words, a verbal attack that flies viciously at him. I am savage and biting, my anger raging brutally against him, yet I am barely conscious of what I'm saying, aware only of the putrid stench of my hateful soul. The raging stops and I drop exhausted on my bunk. I turn stubbornly to the wall with my back turned coldly towards him.

I hear his breaths, deep and even; a steady, quiet rhythm that rises and falls, a gentle undulating song that winds back through my dreams. I float on the lapping tide of his breath as it softly ebbs and flows. I long to crawl into that golden nest of my youth.

I roll over on my hard, cold bed. I strain my eyes towards that corner that purrs with his breathing. The stream of light from the open door stretches towards him but he is still hidden in the shadow. Slowly my eyes adjust and his form gradually emerges from the darkness. He is kneeling on the hard, stone ground, bent over so that his head is bowed right down to the ground. I watch the curved mound of his back rise and fall, the steady motion broken by silent, trembling convulsions that shake his whole, bent body. I stare uncomfortably with a squirming sense of guilt. The minutes pass slowly. At last he lifts his head in a slow but deliberate movement. His shining eyes meet mine and for a second we are joined by an invisible chord that stretches between us. It is too intense and, with a vague sense of shame, I drop my eyes to the floor.

He climbs wearily to his feet. I glance furtively towards him as he straightens and moves with a leaning step towards the door. As the blade of light passes across his face, I feel my breath freeze. Across his face streams rivers of tears that drench his neck and hands, overflowing from the deep lakes of his eyes; tears which run deep red with his own salty blood.

The night passes slowly in a confusion of twisted and broken dreams. I wake frequently, clammy and shivering. I stare into the empty darkness, the strange dreams still luminous and close in my exhausted mind. I try wearily to drive the images away but find myself slipping hopelessly back into sleep, to be tossed and chased and tormented.

The taunting faces are still jeering and shrieking at me when the light goes on in my cell. They crowd around me, hissing and spitting their hate and damnation. I drive my face deeper and deeper into my pillow, to keep them from scratching and tearing at me. They are near to me, poking me sharply in my back, shouting my name. Now they have me, they are shaking me and dragging me from my bed. I wail in fear and pain. "Let me go! Leave me alone!"

Sharp pain cracks my knees as I hit the stone floor. I groan and rub my stinging eyes. Encircling me are three sets of legs, stiff and straight in their prison uniforms.

"Get up. We're here to take you to the warden."

My head throbs as I struggle to orientate myself. Waves of nausea swell in my throat and mingle with the pain from my knees. I feel so heavy and dizzy that I don't know how to move.

"Get up." A heavy boot thuds into my side, forcing the breath from my lungs. I push myself up onto all-fours and suck air into my aching chest. Fear grips me now as I struggle against my weak, flailing limbs and try to stand up. A bitter sense of hopelessness tightens in my throat and swells into a constricting mass of tears. I count each stinging inspiration to calm my swimming head.

The encircling faces stare impatiently as I straighten myself up to their level. Two of them grasp me at either side and almost drag me through the door, my numb feet tripping awkwardly under me. The third marches noisily behind, except at doorways where he moves brusquely to the front to hold the door open. In this way we proceed briskly through the grid of corridors that take us to the warden's office.

My thoughts begin to return to me and I am confused. As my head clears I become surer that I am awake and that this is not still part of my nightmares. But why am I being dragged through the halls of a half-sleeping prison, when I expected to be wakened in the morning to dress for court? Anxiety rings in shrill tones.

I see my lawyer ahead, leaning against the grey-tiled wall. He looks sleepy and strangely informal without his court suit. He stretches his yawning mouth into an odd sort of smile as if he's hoping to reassure me. I am buzzing with alarm. As they march me past him, he reaches out and pats me on the back, still grinning his foolish smirk. I am not reassured. Nothing is happening as it should. They lead me into the warden's office and drop their hold on my limp arms so that I am left standing, loose and awkward, in front of an expansive desk.

A voice tumbles across the room and jolts my paralysed mind. I suddenly notice the figure of the warden sitting behind his desk.

"Sit down."

I stare stupidly back at him with glazed eyes.

"There is a chair behind you. Sit in it."

I slowly grasp the meaning of his words and cautiously look behind me. Seeing a chair, I gingerly lower myself into it and look around. I startle at seeing my lawyer stretched back confidently in the leather armchair beside me, still beaming at me with his silly smile. I look ahead and out of the dim corners of the room I see a whole panel of officials appear.

The warden clears his throat and shuffles through a small pile of papers that lie in front of him on an opened file. He looks about him uncomfortably, as if wondering how to begin.

"The fact is there has been a new development. Something quite unusual; well extraordinary really." He lifts his pile of papers and taps them on his desk before returning them to the file.

My lawyer beside me cannot restrain himself any longer. He slaps his thigh and calls out, "Well get on with it then!" Everyone looks embarrassed. Bewildered, I watch their eyes shift around the room.

The warden coughs again and with a sigh begins his explanation.

My blood runs cold as I hear his words rattle into the waiting room.

The sun strikes my eyes like a sword. I lift my arm to shade my face and squint at the stretching arc of blue that domes me. I feel the heat of the baked earth creep up through the soles of my shoes. The heavy iron gate of the prison closes behind me with a deep clang. Footsteps retreat with snapping steps that echo against the hard stone walls. I am alone in the still, quiet heat. I inhale deeply, wanting to draw the expanse of blue into my tired body. Tiny breaths of breeze blow across my pale face, carrying the sweet smell of sunshine. Lovely warmth spreads through me.

I look furtively behind me. The door is closed and the courtyard empty, but I feel quite insecure, as if the grey-faced building can still swallow me up, its gates swinging open to engulf me. I walk briskly away following the deserted road that leads to the town, keeping my eyes fixed ahead. Anxious thoughts pursue me. What if they realise their error and come after me? My pace quickens almost to a trot. I am too frightened to look behind as I hurry away, longing to increase the distance between me and the prison.

This speed is too much for me. My chest starts to ache with each gasping breath. I slow down, panting and wiping the dripping sweat away from my eyes, stretching my neck forward for air. I peel off my jacket and roll my shirt sleeves up to my elbows. I pull the button free at my neck and loosen my collar. I feel better with a bit of air cooling me. I search my pockets for a handkerchief. Wiping my hot, damp neck and forehead, I glance behind me. I can't see the fortress any more. I scan the space behind me; a stretching, open plain of grass, dotted with trees, dusted with a haze of summer heat. I let my pace ease a little more and allow a small sense of enjoyment to creep into my mind.

The sun inches slowly across the golden sky as I tramp the stony road, eyes fixed ahead on the hazy horizon, the day slipping past me in streams of sunshine.

I hear the distant rumble of a vehicle. Startled, I search the road behind me. I see it moving in a distant dust cloud, creeping along the road. I look anxiously around me. There is nothing but fields; nowhere to hide. The vehicle draws closer, its engine whining its noisy approach. I squint at the moving dust cloud and catch a glimpse of blue. It doesn't look like a prison van. I keep walking.

It roars and bumps until it is close behind me. I keep my eyes straight ahead as it passes by. My heart is leaping dangerously. The car glides away from me and my tension eases.

With a screech, the car suddenly stops. My step falters. With a crunch of gears and a high-pitched whine, the car starts to reverse quickly and recklessly towards me. I freeze, my breath suspended. The car draws beside me, chugging and panting in the heat and dust. I stare at the ground, conscious of the dark, empty window beside me and the scratched and peeling blue paint. A face leans towards the window and calls across.

"Hey! Where are you going?"

"Into town."

"Jump in; I'll give you a ride."

"Thank you but I'll walk."

"Walk!" the driver exclaims. "You're crazy. It's ten miles away and in this heat you'll faint."

Ten miles away! He's right; I won't make that. I swallow, and grip the door handle. "Thank you then. A lift will be great."

The car grinds away and bounces over the rough ground. I stare uncomfortably ahead, watching the ribbon of road disappear under the dented bonnet of the car.

"Are you from around here?"

His voice startles me from my silence.

"No; not from around here," I stammer.

I feel his eyes turn to snatch a look at me, eyes like beams of torch-light sliding over my tense profile. He turns back to the road. I sit in my hot, uneasy silence, wanting the miles to be swallowed up. The car jolts along noisily. Dust stings my nostrils and dries my throat.

"There's a bottle of water at your feet if you're thirsty."

I look down to find a bottle rolling across the floor. It's warm but relieves the thirst that had been swelling my tongue. "Thank you. I didn't realise how much I needed a drink."

I loosen my taut shoulders and let my head drop wearily onto the head-rest behind me. The strange events of the morning flick and run through my mind like a cartoon, scenes jumping and replaying, voices cracked and shrill. I strain to organise the pictures, peering deep into them to see myself. What was I doing? Did I seem shocked? What exactly did he say? The more I concentrate the more the pictures twist away from me and get lost in the shadows that are fogging my mind.

A sudden jerk thrusts me violently forward. I wake in palpitating fear, looking blankly around me, trying desperately to recall what has happened.

"We're here." A smiling voice beams across at me. "You fell sleep and I wasn't sure how far you wanted to go."

I look across to his face and remember winding along the hot road. I try to shake off the drowsy confusion that clings to my mind. His face is folded into a gentle expression of kindness.

"This is my house. I can take you somewhere else if you like, but maybe you'd like a coffee first; to freshen up a bit."

I still feel dazed and nauseous. I sit staring, stupidly; I don't know what to say.

"Come and have a coffee, then you'll feel better. I think you've had a touch too much sun. How long were you out there before I picked you up?"

I can't remember how long I was walking for now; was it hours? The road just stretched on and on, and I just kept running; running away; away from my dread. His kind eyes sway me. I let him lead me into the house.

"The bathroom is through there." I feel his words directing me and obey meekly, walking dumbly down the hall. The bathroom is pastel and perfumed, with plump balls of cotton wool squeezed into an ornamental glass jar. I feel ragged and rough against the floral wallpaper and fussy trims, too used to the harsh, grey walls and steel angles. A face stares at me from the chrome disk of shaving mirror; a pale, haunted face with dark shadows circling the glazed, distracted eyes. I startle to see myself so altered, my thin, bloodless lips quivering at the first sight of such wreckage. I run my hands across the sharp spikes of hair that cap my head.

"Are you hungry? Would you like something to eat?" His voice rouses me from my strange reflection as it calls from the kitchen. I briskly turn the tap and cupping my hands under the cold stream, splash handfuls of deliciously cool water over my face and head, dousing and washing the dust and heat away.

The kitchen is rich with the smells of home and comfort, of coffee brewing and warm toast. Tears swell in my throat and sting my eyes. After months of hard, cold austerity and the hangman dangling his rope over my future, this kindness is confusing; bewildering. He moves back and forth around the kitchen, setting plates and bowls of soup on the table, busying himself with the meal preparations. He seems not to notice my struggling emotions. What is he thinking about me? I must appear strange.

"Please sit down and help yourself." He sits down, inviting me to do the same. I stare at the place set for me, at this generous and completely unexpected offer of hospitality from a stranger, at this overwhelming gesture of kindness and goodness. My head is in a whirl. This meal and this man are everything that is good and kind, and yet I am filled up with cruelty and deception, with the passions of my selfish and insensitive heart. I am frozen in an awkward, silent paralysis; wanting to sit down and be part of this world of goodness; wanting to run away; fearing that his kindness will crumble the stone veneer on my heart, spilling my guilt all over the table.

He looks up at me, as if he knows my struggle, as if he knows me.

In a sudden, wild moment of panic, I spin around and run for the door, rushing outside as if desperate to breathe. I fly down the few steps and throw myself down the street, pounding along the road as fast as I can go. I look back over my shoulder and see him standing at the door, watching. I expect to see anger or surprise on his face, but instead it's just kindness, like I am doing just what he expects me to. I sob as I run, my tears streaming down my wet face, not knowing where I'm going or why I'm running.

I run till I'm breathless and choking, coughing on my tears, pain searing in my chest. The shadows grow long and spill across the street, the sky turns deep and purple like an ink wash; street lights wink and glow in dim circles of light. My feet still struggle forward in a stumbling trot, driven by some unbearable dread, circling through the town but finding nowhere to rest.

The sky is a black velvet cloth, shimmering with a spray of glittering stars. The street is washed in thin, silvery light that trails from the moon. I huddle and watch the last stragglers reel out of the bars and restaurants, and wind their uncertain way home. One by one, the voices fade to a whisper then disappear into the enveloping silence. One by one, darkness snatches the light from each window until only the street lamps are burning. I sit alone in the empty street as it is rustled by the cool early-morning air. Sleep settles like a thick blanket over the town, muffling its movements and sounds. The gleaming moon climbs its course through the heavens. I am still but sleep is far from me. I stretch out on a wooden bench and watch the sky over head, absorbed with its myriad of jewels, waiting for the first light of dawn.

The smooth whir of an engine and several dull thuds interrupt my dreams. I rub my gritty eyes and strain to turn my stiff neck. My body is sore and rigid with cold. I must have fallen asleep. Shivering, I push myself up into a sitting position, head hanging and nauseous.

"Thud!" and another bulky package is dropped onto the pavement from the purring van. Low voices break into the streaky light and the van rolls smoothly away into the grey dawn. A pink haze rims the sky, silhouetting the buildings that crowd the High Street. My stomach is an empty, gnawing pain. I scan the row of shops to look for signs of business. Everything is quiet and still.

I stand up and stretch, feeling quite light-headed. The dizziness passes and I walk with echoing steps up one side of the street, searching the shop-fronts for somewhere to eat. I cross the deserted road and return on the other side. I spy a bakery, but it is still hours until opening time. Beyond it is a newsagent which, I reason, should open earlier and sell snacks of some sort. The pavement is partially obstructed by a large deposit of newspapers. Weak and bilious with hunger, I lower myself onto one of the stacks of papers and wait. I search the street for anyone approaching.

The street murmurs with the distant rumble of car engines, motors which grow louder then fade away. Occasional footsteps snap along the pavement but no-one draws near me. My eyes dawdle across the sheets of newsprint, scanning the blocks of black and white.

"Weather: sunny and dry with cloudy spells; max. 32 degrees Celsius." More hot weather! I need to get a shower really, change my clothes; go home maybe. A shudder passes through my body. A great chasm seems to separate me from my home; from my life. My thoughts start to see-saw again and I push them violently away. My eyes turn to the papers again and I start to read. Drifting down the rows of print, a headline suddenly grips me with horror. My blood freezes as I read the bold black words.

"JUDGE TO BE JUDGED AFTER CONFESSING GUILT "

I quickly scan the article. "A high-court judge will today appear in his own courtroom to face charges of first-degree murder after confessing his guilt in the case he was actually presiding over. The accused in this strange case had been tried and found guilty unanimously by the jury, and was to appear in court for sentencing, when, to the surprise of all involved, he was declared innocent and released from prison in the early hours of yesterday morning. In an unexpected turn around, his father, a well known and respected judge, accepted all guilt for the murder onto himself and secured the pardon for his son. Members of the legal profession are still reeling at this unforeseen revelation. The judge is being detained in the same prison that his son had, until yesterday morning, been a ward of. He will appear in court today for sentencing."

My throat clenches and I exhale with a strangled groan. It must be a mistake. My breath quickens in short pants. I snatch the paper from the pile. There beneath it the same headline glares up at me. I run my eyes over the other papers stacked around me; the story is repeated in every copy. My breath is smacked from my chest. My head is bursting from a great long scream that silently shakes my whole being. What has he done?

Grasping the paper I run away from the shop. Almost blind with fear and panic, I race wildly out of the street, bumping into bins and lamp-posts, not knowing in what direction to flee. The morning light grows brighter and the gloom in the streets lifts. The pavements seem suddenly cluttered with people passing and pressing by. I weave dangerously through them, desperate to get away. I rush along roads littered with shop signs and black bags of rubbish mounded on the kerb, past proprietors pushing up roller doors as they open for trade.

The clutter of commerce becomes gradually sparser and spans out as I find myself racing up the wider, tree-lined streets of the suburbs. My step grows slower as I stumble and stagger breathlessly along. I have to stop. I see an empty bus stop and fall recklessly onto its narrow bench seat, clutching my chest in pain. I bury my throbbing head in my hands and rock with torment. I don't understand. Now they'll hang him in my place.

I stare at the gravel at my feet, my head heavy and hanging. People move about me in a dream; passing, waiting in queues, mounting the shuddering steps of the bus when it arrives with its growling engine and hissing doors. My eyes are fixed on the ground in front of me, my thoughts and senses are closing in, the world around me losing its dimension.

A car engine rumbles quietly, somewhere at the periphery of my awareness. Stones crunch nearby as dirty wheels roll slowly into my narrow field of vision. Familiar blue paint catches my attention. I look up suddenly and see the same battered blue car gliding to a halt in front of me. I stare, dumb and dazed. A cheery voice reaches me as the same man steps out of the car and walks towards me.

"Are you ready for that meal yet?"

"How did you find me?" I stammer.

"I was worried about you. You didn't look well yesterday; you still don't."

He grips me gently but firmly under my arms and steers my staggering body to the car. I find him reassuringly strong and decisive, and submit.

"Right, let's get you home. I think some food and a sleep will go a long way."

I am so weak and tired that I silently eat the food he serves me, and willingly collapse into the bed he offers. My exhausted mind and body immediately tumble into dark oblivion; into floating, falling sleep.

I cautiously open my rough eyes. The sun shines brightly around the room so I quickly snap them shut. Where am I now? I blink my eyes open briefly to see where I am. A clean, tidy but completely unfamiliar room meets my searching eyes. I glance around again and see my clothes folded neatly on a chair nearby, my shoes beneath. I am still confused. I catch sight of my crumpled newspaper and everything floods back with a dreadful, sickening chill. I roll onto my side and bury my face in the bed-covers. The pain is deep and sharp; inescapable.

Muffled noises from the next room remind me that I'm not alone. I shrink into the covers. I can't run away again. His kindness confuses me. Why should he be good to me? Minutes tick by. I don't know what time it is but my stomach is groaning with hunger. I slide out of bed and grab my clothes. They are all clean! I dress quickly and step awkwardly into the hall, following it to the kitchen.

"Hello! Did you sleep well?"

I nod my answer.

"Good. Well help yourself to some lunch. It's all on the table, and the coffee in the pot is fresh. I have to go out now but I'll be back before tea. Make yourself at home. You can stay as long as you like."

I gaze at him, still feeling shy and bewildered, nodding stupidly.

"Err. Thanks for washing my clothes." He just smiles and waves as he leaves. The door bangs shut. His footsteps grow more distant. I'm alone.

I search the room for a clock. It's almost Three O'clock. What day I wonder? How long have I slept for?

I sit down at the small table and pour myself a coffee. I cut off a large chunk of bread and gnaw it hungrily, piling food onto a plate. It all smells and tastes so good that I want to cram it all into my mouth. The sun is streaming in through the window; the breeze is gently lifting the curtains and wafting across my face. It's too unbelievable. I was sitting in a cold, dark cell waiting to die and now....my body shakes and heaves with emotion.

I slowly chew as my elbows press against the neat, checked table-cloth, and let the murmuring sounds of the street wash over me; the distant voices calling and the gentle whine of car engines. The clock ticks steadily, beating the hours. The sun creeps away and I begin to shiver. Clearing the table, I settle in the lounge room, my eyes running over the simple room and the scattering of ornaments. There is little to look at; no photos, a lot of serious-looking books, nothing very personal.

Shadows creep into the room as the sun slides away, filling it with a hovering, waiting sense of gloom. I sit motionless in a deep chair, thoughts drifting with the slowly failing light, with the grey dusk that fills the house. The clock echoes rhythmically, resounding sharply. I am slowly swallowed up in the still, engulfing darkness that clouds and suspends my thoughts; lost in a distant, hazy stare. Only my eyelids move as they drop like a curtain over my absent gaze.

The grating of a key in the lock startles me. I am frozen in the darkness. I listen to the sliding of the door, the approach of footsteps. With a snap the room bursts into light.

"Oh! Sorry. Have I disturbed you?" My host is surprised and apologetic.

I blink and jump to my feet. "No, not at all. I hadn't realised how late it had got." My eyes shift awkwardly around him. I search my empty mind for something to say or do.

"Well, sit down," he says, stepping into the room. "I'll make the tea. You'll have a cup of tea?"

I nod and fold myself obediently into the chair. I listen to the sounds of him moving about in the kitchen; reassuring sounds that soothe me like the hum of a familiar tune; the gentle clink of china cups and the steaming kettle.

A newspaper lies folded on the coffee table. The sight of its crisp, smooth pages jolts my worn emotions with new waves of alarm. I strain to read a date or headline, or even make out a word, but it is impossible. I listen anxiously to the kitchen noises wondering how long I have before he reappears.

The tension is unbearable. I rise quietly from my chair and creep across to the table, quickly unfolding the newspaper. The headline sprawls boldly across the front page. Its heavy print leaps in startling lines of black ink, assaulting my raw eyes. "Judge receives death sentence." I start to scramble through the text, rushing nervously over the words when I sense footsteps in the hall. I hastily restore the paper and drop back into my seat.

He turns into the room balancing a heavy tray; his face beaming. He lowers the tray onto the coffee table, sliding the newspaper out of the way. I watch him as he pours the tea.

"Do you take milk or sugar?"

"Just milk, thank you."

"Strange case this, in the paper today," he continues as he hands me a warm cup of tea and offers a plate of biscuits. "A high court judge sentenced to death."

"For what crime?" I enquire loosely, taking a piece of shortbread.

"Murder, apparently. Quite a nasty case, I believe. Very unpleasant."

"And will he really be executed? There must be some appeal or something, surely." I sip the warm tea and watch his face as he replies.

"No. It seems not. From what I read, anyway. The execution will go ahead. He has made no appeal and accepts the sentence. So it's just a matter of time now."

His face clouds with pain and he lowers it slightly as he struggles with his emotions. I look away, a little embarrassed, perplexed at the intensity of his expression. We both gaze into our cups. The silence presses heavily but my mind is reeling and conversation seems so difficult. I struggle to find something appropriate to say. The pause lengthens awkwardly.

"Have you been following the papers then?" I ask as casually as I am able. My eyes dart across to his face to gauge his response. He has recovered himself and again radiates a warm friendliness and deep composure.

"Well, a bit. Something very odd about it. Seems his son was implicated at first and was tried and found guilty. Then, just as he was about to get the death sentence, the father turned up and said it was really him who was guilty. I don't know? Just strikes me as being odd. To be honest, I still suspect the son."

Dread creeps with cold fingers up my spine but I hold onto my calm appearance.

"Why would the father implicate himself if he wasn't guilty?" I ask breezily.

"To protect his son, of course." His words dart back with steel-like certainty.

I squeeze back into the chair, surprised at the strength of his answer.

He leans towards me with earnest eyes and a quivering mouth. "A good father will sacrifice anything for the son he loves." His words fall heavily from his grave lips.

Heat surges through my cheeks; his words assail me like a sword driving through my heart. My fingers fidget nervously with the arm rest of the chair. He watches my hands with the stillness and concentration of a cat stalking a mouse. I squirm in the heat of his stare, my lips and mind dumb. The clock ticks steadily through the silence.

"I'm sorry; I've made you uncomfortable." His voice breaks suddenly into the silence I was lost in.

"No, not at all," I stammer unconvincingly. "It just seems very extreme; for a father to die in his son's place. If it's true, of course."

"It's true alright," his reply bounds back.

Silence settles uncomfortably around us again until his voice steps softly in.

"A high price to pay, but he is willing. Willing, because someone did it for him once."

"Someone died for my father!" My words fly wildly into the room in a paroxysm of disbelief.

We stare at each other in the naked heat of red-faced exposure. A dumb silence expands in my mind as I grope frantically, stupidly for something to say; some way of covering my blunder. Sweat seeps through the pores of my steaming skin. My throat drums with my racing heart. I sink, loose and dazed, into the soft back of the chair. I am the mouse who is caught, shivering as I await the sharp teeth.

He sits as calm and tranquil as a blue summer sky, his eyes showering me with kindness.

"It's alright," he says at last. "I know who you are. Your father sent me to find you; to look out for you."

My mind is reeling dizzily at his strange, nonsensical words; floundering over his meaning. I gape foolishly at his gentle face.

"It's O.K. I've known all along who you are and what you've done. I'm not going to turn you in. That's not what he wants."

I am limp with astonishment, my strength snatched away by his words. I gaze back at him. "So, what does he want?"

"For you to be free of what you've done, so that you can live; have your life back."

"How can I live after what I've done? Even if they hang him, I'm still dead." My heart hangs like a lead ball, suspended in hopeless futility. My heart is black and cold; numb and lifeless.

"You can live because someone else has already died in your place and He does have the power to give life, and to breathe light and warmth into your heart. He can forgive." His words unfold like neat packages, opened and dropped into my unyielding lap.

In a sudden violent motion, I rise from my chair, enraged, thrusting his words back at him, shoving his kindness into his face, storming, raging. I hear his voice, still gentle, still sweet, trying to rise above my explosion of anger.

"You just need to be sorry; tell Him."

I burst out of the warm, lit room into the shadowy night and run into the cool, enveloping darkness. The light from his open door stretches like a beacon down the black strip of road. His words chase me, abrasive, stinging. I clench my fists over my ears as I run away from them.

"He loves you; that's why." His words echo into the empty street, buffeting against the ringing beat of my shoes as they pound against the pavement, as I run into the dark, empty night.

I stare at the midnight waters that lap the narrow crescent of sandy shore. The surface of the lake spreads in rippling waves of silver and jet beneath the trailing moon. Night always seems to be falling; its long, dusky shadows ending the day with its distractions. Another night stretches ahead, comfortless and cold. My house stands empty and dark behind me, my bed haunted with guilt. I think about him every night at this time. How I did nothing to prevent his death. I'm tired of running; I've been running for so long now; hoping that the night-time shadows will fill my mind and drive away the memory of his face. Weeks have run into months, and I'm tired and worn down. I crawl towards what I have always known but have been running from.

With sobbing cries I call out to the stars that circle His feet, "I'm sorry, Lord, I'm so sorry. Forgive me." I sit, weak and exhausted, but still. I've stopped to rest. The clenching pain eases around my heart and tears fall easily, my breath rising and falling in gentle waves. I can go home now and sleep.

God shows his love for us in that while we were still sinners, Christ died for us.

Romans 5:8

Of Compassion

The early morning hung motionless in misty tones of grey over the squat form of the village church. Thin light strained through the tangled arms of trees as they lifted their bare boughs to the wintry sky, and settled dimly over the church yard, barely casting a shadow. A gravel path wound through the graves, slate-coloured tombstones sinking into the damp and mossy soil, and circled the church building as it huddled in its thick stone walls.

Footsteps crunched in a slow pace up the frosted footpath, and the figure of a man appeared from the gloom. He was huddled into his thick overcoat, sandy hair tufting from his upturned collar; chin buried in the scarf which wrapped him like a shroud. Though still in only his fourth decade, he seemed stooped and shrunken like an older man; his strength and vigour ransacked; his youth plundered. He scraped his feet up to the wrought iron church gates and wearily leant his weight against them. They opened in a stiff arc and he shuffled through.

The churchyard was small and littered with slanting tombstones; inscriptions worn smooth; lichen crawling across the crumbling stonework; small squares of lawn mowed smooth between them. One gravestone stood out in a gleaming contrast of new white marble with sharp-cut edges;

its inscription still bold and clear. Dying flowers were draped limply on its ghostly surface.

The man continued to shuffle his feet along the path as it lead up to the main entrance of the church, then passing the many leaning headstones, he crossed the short distance of lawn till he stood at the foot of his young wife's grave. His head and arms hung numbly as grief coursed violently through his silent body; eyes dry as worn gravestones; lips mute as the chilled morning. The devastation of untimely death pounded against his chest with painful blows.

He stood in the frozen churchyard as light crept silently into the morning and the village started to stir from its sleep.

Crisp steps broke the silence and the clanging of heavy keys echoed around the still churchyard. The man's eyes did not shift from the fresh, white stone. A key turned reluctantly in the lock, and the church doors opened with a grating heave. The dim glow of amber light appeared in each window, giving the illusion of warmth. The man shivered and a fine mist clung to his breath. Silence closed in again.

His solitude was interrupted again by the hum of a car engine. Doors opened and shut, and smart heels clicked up the path. A stream of cars began to fill the narrow street, forming a gleaming queue that hugged the curb, spilling their occupants out into the brisk air. The sparse handful of people grew into a steady flow, and the street and churchyard began to oscillate with busyness.

Ladies clutching patent leather handbags tottered in hats and heels. Men were buttoned up in coats against the flapping wind; Sunday shoes shining and suits pressed. Children kicked and scraped, hanging reluctantly behind, dawdling in a disinterested sprawl. Church bells chimed urgency into their pace and hurried the stragglers, pressing them to the door. The church door opened and shut, snatching them from the cold air and swallowing them up into musty shadows.

The rush of people trailed off to a trickle; the churchyard emptying as suddenly as it had filled. The man still stood motionless at the grave, the tolling bells clanging a discord against his bruised emotions as the last person hurried past him and disappeared through the heavy wooden door. The chiming and scurry of footsteps ceased; the ring of salutations melted away. Silence spread through the gravestones. He hugged his coat closer as a faint stream of sunlight struggled to bring warmth.

Time passed slowly, punctuated by the muffled strains of chorus and organ as they escaped the fortified church walls.

In a sudden moment the doors burst open and the congregation rushed past him as a surging wave, streaming towards the gate. Laughter rang and shrieked as children raced and skidded dizzily between the graves, scattering stones from the path, jostling against their parents. Some people lingered in cloistered tête-à-têtes; others left with a brisk handshake. The cars eased cautiously from the curb and rolled smoothly away.

Bell-like, a child's voice rose above the hum and chatter in ringing clarity.

"Mummy, isn't that Mr. Burns standing over there? He looks so sad."

A hushed voice replied. "Yes, I know darling, but you mustn't stare at people."

An embarrassed strain fell over the conversations as people hurried to conclude and depart. The crowd quickly melted away.

The man trembled with an added pain as the crowd washed away, abandoning him to his silence; his utter isolation. The wind whipped sharply around him and moaned through the over-hanging trees. The graveyard was again wrapped in silence and stillness.

At the other side of the grave, unseen by everyone, crouched the figure of another man. He was wrapped lightly in a length of white linen cloth and bowed over in grief. His face was etched with sorrow; his eyes raw with tears. He too was silent. He seemed unaware of the cold, despite his inadequate dress; nor was he wearied by his uncomfortable vigil. His face, swollen with love, gazed down at the grave, but every few moments he would cast his eyes upwards and study the other man's face, bringing fresh contortions of pain onto himself. And so he crouched, weeping and watching over them both; husband and wife.

The husband shuffled his feet, and with a despairing look, edged away from the graveside, moving as if to leave. As he did so, the crouching man stretched his hand up towards him and stood, reaching fervently out to him. The white linen garment slid away from his extended arm. His hands and feet were pierced and bloody, and a stream of blood flowed from his wounded side.

GLIMPSES

Beyond the Clouds

Your face is warm with colour, reaching through the whiteness; soft eyes, swimming with pain, that grab at my wavering heart. Every detail and line is lost in the whiteness except your face which is holding me here; a face swollen with longing, bent over me in grief.

I don't want to leave you; bone of my bones, flesh of my flesh.

I am as thin and blanched as this death-room bed-linen; you are ruddy with life, your kiss still warm, your hand smooth on my bony cheek. How I have loved your face and gentle hands; but I have been hanging for too long in the grey ebb of sickness, watching life grow in you.

I am a girl smiling in nuptial white as spring daffodils are a sea of bobbing yellow. The breeze, still freshened by snow, startles my skin and tosses my skirts as I dash laughingly into the church. People rise solemnly, ceremonially in their pews, but I search for the darkness of your eyes, glistening in the smooth curve of your face; a face pale with youth and apprehension. I am not afraid as I lunge towards you, the mystery of your eyes, the kindness of your smile and the uncertainty of our years together. I grasp your hand and shelter in its large, firm hold; so smooth.

"Enjoy yourself, Lassie! You're only a bride for a day, and a wife for life!"

A rather hurried and distracted bride, I wanted to be a wife.

Daffodils burst through the grey in dancing colour, and I'm drenched in the sweetness of our first kiss, and the clear blue of an April sky as it reaches towards the sun.

His body hangs from the rough wood, contorted by pain, streaked by blood and tears; chest rasping slow, painful breaths, as He slumps against His nails. Darkness closes over the midday sun.

"Father, into your hands I commit my spirit." He breaths his last. It is done.

A woman watches from a distance, her face blanched with horror. Nausea courses in violent waves through her frail form. She gasps and cries out as His flesh is hammered and torn. Tears spill out of her eyes as she cleaves to the sight of Him. She hears His cry, His last cry, and clutching herself, sinks to the ground moaning.

Her mind echoes with her own cry as she rocks and wails, "No! No! No! You can't take Him. I love Him. I love Him."

A sea of people wash by her, bewildered, disturbed. She rocks and wails, pain like a knife blade tearing her breast; tears choking her.

"No!" Her cry is lost in the darkness and terror.

She remains crouched in the strange darkness as His body hangs, limp with death, until sunset.

She sees two men approach the guards, their arms waving in passionate pleas, thrusting the official papers forward urgently. She strains to see their faces, kind faces but obscured. A whisper passes amongst the women; it is Joseph, a good man, a councillor. The guards pull the body roughly to the ground and the two men take Him gently in their arms. They wrap Him in linen and carry Him away to a tomb they have made ready for Him. The woman follows, her frightened eyes grasping hold of everything that happens.

The men strain together against the great stone, inching it across the opening of the tomb, urgent to secure His body from the watching guard. The woman watches the dark opening of His burial place being slowly eclipsed by the huge boulder, shivering as their separation is sealed in stone.

"Do you take this man to be your lawfully wedded husband; to have and to hold, to love and to cherish, to honour and obey; for better or for worse, for richer or for poorer; in sickness and in health; for as long as you both shall live?"

"I do."

She huddles in grief as His cross lifts its empty arms up to heaven.

I wake in a room glinting with early morning light as it filters through the pale blue curtains and gently touches us in our bridal bed. Our first morning sparkles with sunshine. I nestle against the warmth of your sleeping form as it rises and falls with dreaming breaths, and gaze at the new band of gold which circles my finger. Heat quietly steals through my cheeks. I draw in the cool morning air to still my dancing heart.

First light streaks the dawn in pale beams; the women venture nervously into the empty streets. Faces stained and swollen with burning tears and sleepless nights, they huddle together, clutching their jars of spices. Her pounding heart throbs noisily through her neck and mind; driving her thoughts.

"Who will move the great stone? I have to see Him. I won't be able to move it myself - too heavy for all of us. But I have to get to Him; see Him; touch Him. What if the guards won't let us? What will we do then? They must let us. What if they arrest us for being with Him? I must see Him; must see Him."

She hurries through the gloom, pressed by her heart, urgent with longing; her eager eyes searching ahead for the sight of His tomb.

The air is suddenly smacked from her lungs and blood drains away from her frightened face. She steps cautiously forward with darting, uncertain eyes. The stone has been rolled away from His tomb; it's open. Confusion crashes through her mind and she runs towards the dark, gaping hole. She braces herself against the dry, rough stone, then stoops to look in; breath heaving, eyes squinting. Alarm shrieks through her mind and veins.

"No! This can't be!" Her hands clasp her trembling mouth and clenched stomach. She runs her eyes over the empty strips of linen as they lie folded in on themselves. He's gone. She collapses onto the stony ground outside His tomb and breaks into tears that shake her whole frail, folded body.

"Woman, why are you weeping?" A gentle voice rouses her.

Blinking, she looks up into a man's face. Her own voice struggles to answer.

"Because they have taken my Lord away and I don't know where He is."

A faint note of hope springs into her words. "Do you know where He is? Have you carried Him away somewhere? Tell me where you have put Him and I'll get Him."

A passionate smile spreads quietly through the man's face.

"Mary!" He calls softly to her.

Her eyes widen with recognition as she looks up to Him again.

"Rabbi!" she cries. With drenched face she scrambles towards Him; warm, salty tears bubbling over her smiling face. Laughing and crying, she kneels at His feet, hugging His legs, pressing the hem of His tunic to her pursed lips. Tears streak His dusty feet as she holds onto Him; holds Him, never wanting to move from His feet.

Hands gently smoothing her hair, He steps backwards and draws away from her. Pain flashes across her face; His eyes meet her anguish.

"Not yet, Mary. Don't cleave to me yet. I am not yet ascended to the Father. Go and tell the others what you have seen. Go quickly."

His face soothes and strengthens her as He urges her to go. She pulls herself away and begins to run, feet flinging themselves over the rocky path, mind rushing chaotically ahead. She pounds breathlessly at the heavy door, leaning her weight on the solid timbers; chest heaving. Her fist beats against the portal again and again. Blood rushes in a frantic scream through her mind and pulses noisily in the morning stillness.

"Open the door," she breaths and drums the door in agitation.

The door inches open reluctantly, cautiously revealing a shadowy slither of face. Frightened eyes peer at her. She stares back in unblinking silence. Words struggle into order and splutter into the unyielding doorway.

"He is risen!"

Bed-clothes tangle me as light cuts through the curtains that frame the sprawling branches of the tree. I stare, searching the panes of sky. The stretch of grey inches brighter. The tree is still, its scrabble of dead branches scratching against the veil of pale grey; scrawling lines that cut up and fragment the upper panes of my window.

Weak light settles on the stretching planes of wall, wrinkling the draped mounds of clothes left slung on the back of a chair, rummaging through the scattered papers. The morning creeps along the empty lines of the mantle piece, glancing over its scanty trail of dispossessed objects, barely leaving a shadow. The mirror gazes passively at the featureless spread of the ceiling. A dull gloom hangs in the corners and clings to the day.

Time hovers; stilled by the inertia of the room, dragged forward by the cycle of sounds that move around me.

There was a brief awakening, when the piping clock roused me from melting dreams and I reached across the crumpled folds of our bed to touch you. Your eyes were dark and shiny in the half-light; your skin smooth and young, with the clinging scent of night.

With the splashing of water, the night is washed away. You are bright with cold clothes and combed-smooth hair; crouching at my side to say good-bye.

Alone, I search for sleep as it creeps away from the penetrating light.

The house moves with other people's lives. Breakfast explodes above me with a rush of feet and scrape of chairs; noises cutting suddenly into the heavy silence. A torrent of children bang happily down the stairs with school bags and ringing calls. I follow their footsteps, knowing the sound of each door as it opens and shuts. The postman heaves his van up to the door; skids over the gravel drive and grinds up the hill, his motor winding away between the trees.

Outside is frozen in silence, like an old film, flickering inaudibly. Clouds trail across the sky, leaves curl with the amber tones of Autumn. Crows pick and stalk across the empty lawns; a squirrel scampers daringly.

How long have I lain here, shrouded in the sallow grey of illness? I was white lace and brocade, dazzling with hope, grasping the new spring sunshine; a crumpled leaf unfolding in shy, transparent green, wavering expectantly. I didn't flourish with the season, but shivered and waned; shrinking, wasting. Summer passed in a brief arc of the sun; grasses ripened in a swaying screen; fruit hung heavily, gorged in sweetness. Autumn crept through and stole the summer green while I lay wrapped in a sprawl of blankets.

Stillness. The afternoon sun no longer stretches across my bed. The grey mist has settled around me. Nausea pervades my mind; fever and pain hang stubbornly onto my limbs. Weakness, my body grows weary.

I still gaze at the square of sky, hope ebbing away into the shifting monochrome. I look for a face to break the endless waiting, the grinding agony of each long day. Tears swell and press against my sick heart.

You are a golden hope which lies warm and steady in my restless heart; a glint of spring peeping through the winter grey that stretches ahead. You are with me always.

Dust dances in curling clouds around the feet of the men as they walk briskly; their voices trailing in a low murmur. She follows quietly at a distance; shrinking, hesitating; trying not to be seen. Apprehension pulls tightly at her stomach. The men are absorbed in their conversation and don't look around. Her thoughts drum impatiently. "I always followed before, when Jesus was here. Why shouldn't I come now?" The path winds slowly through the dusty heat and dry pastures; sheep bleat distractedly as they meander over the slopes dotted with bleached boulders.

The men slow down as the path steepens; she holds herself back, pausing a little, hovering by a rocky outcrop. She snatches pieces of their conversation, words which tumble down the slope.

"But He told us to meet him here."

"Are you sure that's what He said?"

"Of course."

"Why?" she asks herself. "What's He going to do now?"

She draws her arm across her damp forehead. Waiting until the men have disappeared over the brow of the hill, she presses on up the hill. Gravel crunches under her feet as she climbs wearily to the summit, the heat rising in waves off the baked ground.

A cool breeze plays lightly around her face as she climbs the last part of the steep slope, relieved to see the ground level off. Her heart dances with anticipation. She lowers herself onto the ground, sinking gratefully into the springy grass, and looks around.

Ahead she can see the men stop. Like a dipping wave, they all drop to their knees and bend their foreheads to the ground. She strains her eyes to see what is happening. She feels her weariness fall away as she catches sight of a figure standing beyond the men. She springs lightly to her feet and crouching, she moves nimbly forward, her eyes still fixed on the white figure.

As she creeps forward she can hear the men's voices rising and falling in praise as the wind catches their words and tosses them over the mountain top. His voice glides smooth and clear like a sword, cutting through the flapping breeze, the drifting sheep calls and the singing worship. Her heart jumps as she recognizes His voice. She stops and searches for His eyes. They are dark pools drawing her closer. She runs to be nearer as He talks to the men, urging, explaining; her burning ears drinking in His precious thoughts.

His white robes billow softly in the growing breeze as He speaks. The sharp stones press into her knees as she bows before Him, the dust swirling into her eyes. She tilts her head to keep her eyes joined to His. He seems to be moving upwards; she lifts her head further. His feet are gliding up through the air before her; she jumps to her feet as the hem of His tunic sails over her head. His voice cascades down as the clouds begin to drift like a translucent veil over His floating form.

"I am with you always. Even to the end of time."

"Always," she repeats. "He is with me always."

She stares upwards as white clouds hide Him from her, clutching onto His words.

I am a young child, floating on the warm grass under the spreading arches of a Jacaranda sky. Birds lilt and sail across my sleepy gaze, their voices a distant "caw-caw" which lulls my dreamy thoughts. My eyes wander lazily after the drifting clouds, squinting around the hazy edges of the burning sun. Heat passes in soothing waves across my basking form, fanned by the gentle, wafting breeze. I shelter in the dreamy stillness of the day, the simple happiness and ease. Summer surrounds me in a dull hum.

In one sliding second the warmth is eclipsed; the sun swallowed up by a cloud. A shiver passes through my startled skin. I sit up and search the heavens. Tears rush into my gaping eyes.

"Mama, the sun has gone. Why did it go away when I was so happy?"

She smiles. "It's still there, darling. It's just hidden by the clouds."

Hot tears burn silent streams across my cheeks, and lie cold and damp on my pillow. Grief swells up as a nauseous pain and throbs through my clenched throat. The empty sky stares passively down; a blanket of cloud; unyielding; silent. I stare back, searching; hope sinking.

Frustrated longing grips each long day as it stretches towards darkness. The room swims and blurs through a salty screen of tears.

"I want to see His face."

His eternal words whispers to me, "I am with you always."

I strain through the mist to hold onto your face, as the whiteness obscures and carries you away. I wrestle in nauseous effort, flailing hopelessly against the enveloping white.

"Where have you gone?" A last frightened sob breaks out from my aching heart, and I let go.

I am melting into the whiteness, pain and nausea evaporating away, floating on the songs of angel voices; music ringing in transcendent strains.

A low, gentle note reaches across the heavens as the last trumpet is blown.

I am dazzling white, swirling in a perfect dome of deep ocean blue, dotted with a host of stars. I am veiled as a bride, trailing in soft robes of clean white; draped in silver purity.

The stars sparkle and swell as they clamour together. We are a multitude of smiling brides, whispering joyfully, expectantly. We rustle and shimmer in new gowns, soft voices stirring musically.

"He is coming; He is coming. And I will see His face."

"For now we see in a mirror, dimly; but then face to face."

1 Corinthians 13:12

Also by the same author

The award winning title "His Name is Love"

Joseph crouched immobile in front of the charred, burning ruin of his home as the ebony sky slowly faded into the dawn. The sick ball of pain squeezing his throat broke into hot, rolling streams of tears that tumbled down his face.

"Help me," he cried. "Someone please help me."

Who is the mysterious stranger that responds to Joseph's desperate cry, meeting him in the agony of loss, loving him through his darkness and confusion, and gilding his life with hope?

This simple story, woven with light and hope, reveals how one man's sacrifice brings new life to many and will appeal to teens and adults alike.

His Name is Love
ISBN: 0954882105

Available at all good bookshops!
www.latentpublishing.com